"I'm not in the market for a guy,"

Honey told Andy.

"Well, I'm not in the market for a gal, either."

Their gazes locked. He swayed toward her almost imperceptibly, but enough to quicken her thudding heart rate. "We've both learned our lessons," she said. "We both know better."

"Yes," he agreed. "We know better…."

As his voice trailed off, Honey had to close her eyes for a moment to block out the sight of his mouth, so kissably close. So damned kissably close.

"We're only human, Andy," she said with a sigh. "We've both loved and been loved. It's only natural that we might be tempted now and then."

"Only natural," he echoed.

"But we're too smart to give in to it."

"Much too smart," he said.

And then he kissed her.

Dear Reader,

Where's the best place to find love this holiday season? UNDER THE MISTLETOE! This month, Silhouette Romance brings you a special collection of stories filled with spirited romance and holiday cheer.

'Tis the season for Christmas wishes, and nine-year-old Danny Morgan has a tall order. He wants to reunite his divorced parents. Will FABULOUS FATHER Luke Morgan be able to win ex-wife Sherri Morgan's love—and fulfill his son's dreams? Find out in Carla Cassidy's heartwarming romance, *Anything for Danny.*

Helen R. Myers brings us a wonderful romance about the power of true love. *To Wed at Christmas* is David Shepherd and Harmony Martin's wish—though their feuding families struggle to keep them apart.

Linda Varner continues the trilogy, MR. RIGHT, INC. with *Believing in Miracles.* Falling in love again may be out of the question for single dad Andy Fulbright. But when he meets Honey Truman, *marriage* isn't....

Look for more love and cheer with a charming book from Toni Collins. *Miss Scrooge* may not have much Christmas spirit, but it's nothing that a holiday with sexy Gabe Wheeler can't cure. Lucinda Lambert is running from danger when she finds protection and love in the arms of *A Cowboy for Christmas.* Look for this emotional romance by Stella Bagwell. And Lynn Bulock rounds out the month with the delightful *Surprise Package.*

Wishing you a happy holiday and wonderful New Year!

Anne Canadeo
Senior Editor

Please address questions and book requests to:
Silhouette Reader Service
U.S.: 3010 Walden Ave., P.O. Box 1325, Buffalo, NY 14269
Canadian: P.O. Box 609, Fort Erie, Ont. L2A 5X3

BELIEVING IN MIRACLES

Linda Varner

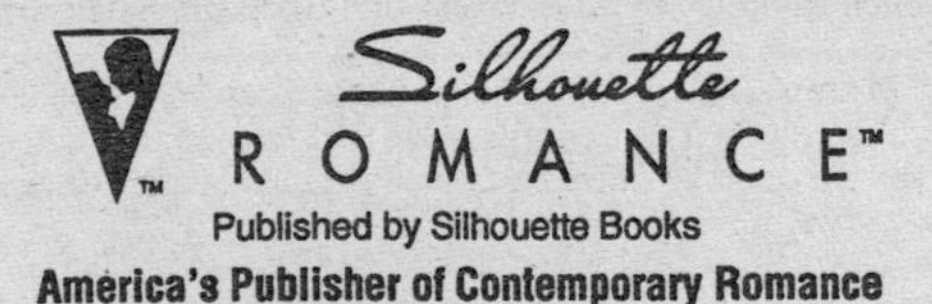

ISBN 0-373-19051-4

BELIEVING IN MIRACLES

This edition published by arrangement with Harlequin Enterprises B.V.

Printed in U.S.A.

Books by Linda Varner

Silhouette Romance

Heart of the Matter #625
Heart Rustler #644
Luck of the Irish #665
Honeymoon Hideaway #698
Better To Have Loved #734
A House Becomes a Home #780
Mistletoe and Miracles #835
As Sweet as Candy #851
Diamonds Are Forever #868
A Good Catch #906
Something Borrowed #943
Firelight and Forever #966
**Dad on the Job* #1036
**Believing in Miracles* #1051

*Mr. Right, Inc.

LINDA VARNER

definitely believes in love at first sight. "But Jim and I were only in ninth grade when we fell, so a whirlwind courtship was definitely out of the question!" Today, she remains happily married to her junior high school sweetheart, and they live in their Arkansas hometown with their two children.

Carpenter Andy Fulbright On Building The Perfect Marriage:

Building a marriage is like building a house. You must have a sensible blueprint, good supplies and the right tools.

Blueprints are easy. Just remember the mistakes you made last time you built it and adjust your plan accordingly. As for supplies, one man and one woman are all that's necessary—either or both can come equipped with a child, too.

Tools are *most* important. There are some you should definitely use: patience, compassion and honesty. There are some you must avoid: arrogance and pride.

Oh, and there's one other thing you'll definitely need—a good foundation. But whatever you do, never build your marriage on love...unless her hair is the color of spun honey, that is.

Chapter One

"You must be Andy Fulbright—the carpenter who's going to make the bookcases."

"Yes," Andy replied to the blond-haired woman sitting cross-legged on the floor at his feet. Hundreds of books were strewn all around her in this empty bedroom of Albert Winter's former guest house. Boxes filled with even more of them lined the walls. "And you're..."

"Honorine Truman, the librarian." She extended her right hand as she introduced herself.

Struck dumb by her modern good looks, Andy barely had wits to take and shake her hand. He then forgot to let it go, busy, instead, with assessing her oversize burgundy sweater, matching leggings and ankle boots.

Not bad, he decided, and *not* the bespectacled spinster he'd instantly envisioned upon learning that a Boston librarian would be in charge of cataloging the books ol' man Winter had willed to the town of Winterhaven, Alabama.

"Do I pass?" she asked, tugging her fingers free of his. She sounded a bit annoyed by his blatant inspection.

Andy started guiltily. "I'm staring."

"You are."

"Sorry. It's just that you're a, um, challenge to a few of my preconceptions."

"Marian, Madam Librarian?"

"Exactly," Andy admitted, immediately recognizing her reference to a song from *The Music Man* that perfectly described the stereotypical librarian he'd expected.

She forgave him with a shrug that dropped the scoop neck of her sweater off one peachy tan shoulder. "That's okay. You don't look like a carpenter, either."

"And just what does one look like?"

Honorine Truman didn't have to think twice. "Skin-tight jeans, muscle shirt and the pecs to go with it, leather tool belt bulging with—"

"Enough! Enough!" Andy winced and held up both hands to silence her. "I get the picture." And it wasn't a pretty one... at least to him.

At once self-conscious, he finger combed his short black hair, a gesture picked up last year when he realized he'd inherited the Fulbright receding hairline.

"Are you looking for Nicole?" Honorine asked, reaching for a thick blue book, obviously heavy, which she set on her lap and opened.

"Yes. I was supposed to meet her here at 9:00."

"It's 9:45."

Andy glanced at his watch. "So it is."

"She waited thirty minutes for you." Huge green eyes scolded him before she shifted her attention to the book and began to thumb through it.

"I had another job that took longer than I expected," he said by way of explanation, even though he owed her none at all. Her response irritated him just a little. "Am I supposed to call her or what?"

"Mmm-hmm," Honorine replied, an answer that revealed nothing except that she had work to do and probably wouldn't even notice if he exited.

Accepting his dismissal with good enough grace—he had work to do, too—Andy backed out of the room and walked down the hall to the kitchen, as bereft of furnishings as the rest of the house. From there he telephoned Nicole Winter, fiancée of one of his partners. She'd hired him to make the wooden bookshelves needed to transform this empty guest house into a public library.

"Yo, Nicole," he greeted her when she answered. "Sorry I missed you this morning, but I got hung up on another job."

"Marcie Mabry's pet door?"

"How'd you know that?"

"I called Ethan when you didn't show up at 9:00. Was *Miz* Mabry her usual charming self?"

"And then some," Andy answered with a heavy sigh. Marcie, freshly divorced and on the prowl, called at least once a week with a project for him, and since his partnership in Do It Right, Inc. was so new, he couldn't really afford to turn down work. "After I cut the door to her specifications, she told me she wanted it bigger."

"So you had to recut?"

"That's right, and then she decided she liked the first size best."

Nicole clucked her tongue in sympathy. "Bless your heart. How'd you get out of that one?"

"I pointed out that while her poodle has room to spare, a bigger dog would still have a problem getting in the house."

"But she hates big dogs."

"True, but as I also pointed out, most men like them, and a single woman as attractive as she would be smart to plan ahead."

"You silver-tongued devil! What'd she say?"

"She asked me what kind of dog *I* had," Andy admitted with some embarrassment. Since moving to Winterhaven back in May, he'd been hired to do an astonishing variety of carpentry jobs for an amazing number of single women, each as aggressive as Marcie.

Nicole hooted with laughter. "Watch out, Andy Fulbright, or you'll be the next handyman celebrating an engagement."

"I'll celebrate Christmas in July before I do anything that stupid," Andy retorted, reminded of the party she and Ethan had thrown to announce their planned nuptials. Divorced and admittedly bitter toward his ex-wife, who now lived in France with their daughter, Andy had spent the whole party biting his tongue to keep from quoting the current divorce rate to his starry-eyed friends. "Er, not that I think you and Ethan are stupid...."

"Uh-huh." Nicole's tone of voice told him she knew exactly what he really thought.

"I just don't have time for dating games right now. I've got lots and lots of bookshelves to build so you can get through with this renovation." Converting the guest house into a library was the final phase of a two-phase project. Phase one, almost complete, consisted of remodeling Albert Winter's mansion and grounds into a sort of community center for the good citizens of Winterhaven.

"And speaking of the renovation...did you meet Honey, my librarian?"

Honey? Andy grinned his delight with the nickname, which exactly matched the color of Honorine's hair. "I met her."

"What'd you think?"

"I thought she was—" in rapid-fire succession one adjective after another sprang to mind, like sexy, gorgeous, intriguing, among others "—nice."

"Oh, she is. We've been friends for years, you know. Met at Boston State."

"Really?" Tell me more... tell me more.

"But you don't want to hear about our crazy school days."

"Hey, talk as long as you like," Andy smoothly replied, his tone deliberately light. "You're the boss."

"And you have much to do." She then proceeded to share some last-minute inspirations on the library project, and ended the conversation with a reminder. "The lumber and whatever else you ordered are on the back deck. Dad's notes and sketches are there on the bar just in case you need them. Any questions, call Ethan."

"Call Ethan? Are you telling me you talked him into taking over for you?"

"Well, I am a little preoccupied with our wedding," she said with a laugh, adding, "isn't he a sweetheart?"

"That's one word for it, I guess," Andy replied and then hung up on her before she could hang up on him.

Whistling again, he walked across the kitchen to the patio door, which he slid open and stepped through. After sliding the screen door across to keep insects out of the house, Andy breathed in the crisp November air and enjoyed the view of the Talladega Mountains off to the north. It looked as though Mother Nature had dipped her paintbrush in a rainbow and flung color all over them.

The trees surrounding the guest house were just as beautiful, and while Andy could've stood there for hours in appreciation, he quickly turned his attention to the top-quality pine the lumberyard had stacked on the deck.

Beside the boards lay a box filled with nails, screws, wood glue, sandpaper, stain and all the other paraphernalia he'd need. At once, Andy experienced a rush of emotion that was one part anticipation and three parts relief. The lumber meant steady work; steady work meant he could avoid the single women of Winterhaven, who were a temptation to him despite his earnest claims to the contrary.

He was only human, after all, and lonely as hell.

"Oh, there you are." To Andy's amusement, Honey did just what he'd done the moment she slid the screen door aside and stepped out onto the deck—sucked in a lungful of fresh air. "Mmm. I just love autumn."

"My favorite time of year."

She smiled at him. "I'm making coffee. Want some?"

"Sure."

Andy watched until Honey disappeared back into the kitchen, his appreciative gaze on her long legs and the curve of her derriere, which was almost indiscernible thanks to the bulky sweater, but still unmistakably female. With a rueful shake of his head, he jumped off the deck and headed around the corner of the house to his truck, parked out front. Then he moved the vehicle to the back to unload it. Minutes after that, the crowded deck resembled a carpentry shop, complete with the various tools and materials necessary to accomplish the task of transforming plain old boards into versatile, sturdy bookcases.

Andy silently thanked Albert Winter for not only his vision, but for his attention to detail, too. If the man hadn't left so many specific instructions for his daughter, she'd probably have bought metal shelving, thereby cheating Andy of this opportunity to do what he loved best—create beautiful furniture.

One eye on the door through which Honey would return any moment, and one eye on his "shop," Andy strapped on his tool belt and toyed with the idea of shedding his heavy flannel shirt, in hopes of animating Honey's vision of a carpenter.

And why not? He worked out three times a week and wasn't ashamed of his body. Why, she might be so overcome by the glorious sight that she'd...

What? Andy asked himself with a snort of disgust. Shed her own clothes? And if she did, then what?

"Do you take it sweet?"

Sweet, hot and often, he silently replied, the next instant giving himself a brisk mental shake. "Black, please."

At once, she handed him a steaming mug of coffee. "That should warm you up."

Much more than warm already, Andy just nodded and sipped his drink, thankful for the tool belt that hid the all-too apparent result of his foolhardy fantasies.

"Are you going to work out here?" Honey asked, clearly innocent of his inappropriate thoughts and regretful physical response to them. "I mean—well, I take breaks on this deck, but it is kind of cool for an extended stay."

"Once I get started working, I'll be sweating. In fact—" he couldn't resist saying it "—I'll probably have to lose this shirt. Want me to call you when I do?"

She sighed and pressed a hand to her heart, eyelids fluttering as though overcome by the very thought. "Oh, please."

Andy laughed then, set down his empty mug, and bent to retrieve one of the boards. Ever conscious of her gaze, he balanced it on the sawhorse and then got busy measuring, marking and sawing it to the specifications on the plans he'd drawn from Albert's meticulous notes.

Saying not a word, Honorine sat on the railing that framed the deck, her gaze now on the lawn or maybe the mansion a few yards farther down the drive.

Thanks to the safety glasses he wore, Andy was able to sneak more than one look at her ring finger, but never could make a decision on her marital status. Not that it mattered, he told himself. He'd treat her the same either way. Lustful imaginings aside, he really didn't intend to do anything—as in befriend, date or sleep with a woman—that might expose him to heartache.

He'd already suffered more than his share.

"You guys did a beautiful job on the big house," Honorine suddenly commented. "Nicole took me through it last night and I—" Abruptly she halted. "Does my talking bother you?"

"No." Andy picked up a second board and positioned it on the sawhorse.

"Good. I wouldn't want to be a distraction. I know you've got a lot to do."

A distraction? If she only knew.

"Anyway...the house is perfect and so are the gardens. Ethan's very talented, isn't he?"

"Yes. He owned a successful landscaping business in St. Louis before he moved back here."

"So Nicole said." Honorine took another sip of her coffee. "She also said that you and, um, what's your other partner's name, the electrician?"

"Jack Austin."

"Oh, yeah... Jack. I haven't met him yet. Nicole said that both you and Jack had your own businesses, too, in other states, and that the three of you had always talked about forming a partnership and finally just moved back home and did it."

"That's right," Andy murmured, though it was only a half truth. In reality, each man had diverse personal reasons for moving back to Winterhaven. The partnership was more a lucky by-product of them.

"I think that's really cool." Honorine glanced at her watch. "Oops. I've got to get back to work." She stood and reached out a hand. "Finished with your coffee?"

"Yes, but you don't have to wait on me," he said, nonetheless handing her his empty mug. "I'm used to taking care of myself, and I'm pretty handy in the kitchen, by the way."

"Is that so?"

"Yes."

"Then tomorrow *you* get to make the coffee." That said, she gave him a smile and a wave, then vanished indoors.

Tomorrow. Andy liked the sound of that as well as the thought of the two of them alone in the house for as long as it took to do what had to be done. Target completion date for opening the library was six months. He'd have his part finished before that, of course, but it would probably take Honey that much time and maybe more to catalog all those books by herself. With those thoughts still in the back of his mind, Andy worked at a leisurely pace the rest of the morning, focusing not on speed but on delivering a quality product.

Sometime around noon, Honey stuck her head out the door long enough to say she was leaving for lunch, an announcement that killed any unacknowledged hopes he had that the two of them might get a hamburger somewhere nearby and eat together. It was probably just as well, Andy decided, a little surprised that he'd even considered such a possibility. He drove to a corner grocery store, ordered a sandwich of bologna, salami, summer sausage and cheese, which they made for him at the meat counter, then ate it in his car, his thoughts still on Honey.

What was it about her that attracted, instead of repelled, him as all the other women in Winterhaven had done? Sure, she was a looker, but good-looking females were a dime a dozen today thanks to makeup, beauty shops and fashion magazines. Of course Honorine's skin did radiate the sort of natural glow not available at a cosmetic counter, and her hair, worn long and loose, didn't have much style to it. As for her clothes, they were nice, but not especially glamorous. And still the woman had class.

Maybe it's the iffy state of her marital status that intrigues me, Andy mused. Knowing she might be safely married, and therefore not a real temptation, had probably done wonders for her appeal.

Andy suddenly nodded and murmured, "Yeah," around a bite of sandwich. That was it. That had to be it. Deep inside, he believed that any woman as attractive as Honorine had to be taken already. Therefore he didn't feel threatened when he was around her.

* * *

One o'clock found Andy back at the guest house. A quick check of the place revealed that Honorine wasn't back yet.

He went to work immediately and was so involved in his task that he wasn't even aware when Honey returned. Around two o'clock, however, she walked out onto the deck and sat as long as her break allowed, about fifteen minutes.

Honey said little. Andy said less. But the emotional climate was as friendly as that morning's, he thought. Alone on the deck once more, Andy measured and sawed for another couple of hours, at which time he heard, of all things, a child's voice.

"Mama! Mama!"

The sound so startled Andy that he dropped his tape measure. Bending to retrieve it, he heard a door slam inside the house and felt the deck vibrate slightly beneath his feet as though someone—maybe two or even three someones—was running through the house.

Curious, he walked to the door and peered through the screen into the kitchen. He saw nothing, but heard plenty.

"How was your first day at kindergarten? Did you have fun? Did you make new friends?" The voice was Honey's and filled with undeniable excitement, unmistakable love.

"Uh-huh." Probably a boy. A young boy.

"And did you wait where I told you this afternoon?"

"Travis waited exactly where you told him." Andy recognized Nicole's voice this time. "The four of us stopped for a shake on our way home. We brought shakes for you and Andy... he's still here, isn't he?"

"Out on the deck, I think," Honey said.

"Romy, take this to your Uncle Andy, will you?" Nicole's request, loud and clear, prompted Andy to scuttle back to work so he wouldn't appear to be eavesdropping.

In seconds, the screen door was pushed aside with a bang. "Hi, Uncle Andy," said Romy, who wasn't really Andy's niece at all, but Ethan's thirteen-year-old daughter. She stepped out onto the deck, followed by Kyle, Ethan's two-year-old son, and another boy, undoubtedly this Travis. "We brought you a surprise."

"Why, thanks, babe." He reached for the shake and took a long sip, noting that it was slightly warm, but delicious all the same. "Who's your friend?"

"Travis Truman. He's five. He belongs to Honey."

Andy now realized with a sharp stab of what could only be disappointment that Madam Librarian was married... very married. And he could sleep better at night knowing he was safe from the temptation of her charms.

Damn the luck.

"Hi, Travis. My name is Andy Fulbright. It's nice to meet you." Andy reached out his right hand. Travis, with no hesitation, did the same and shook it. Andy noted that the child had his mother's mouth and nose, but that his onyx hair and eyes were definitely someone else's, as was his olive complexion. To Andy's amazement, he felt another stab, this time of unmistakable jealousy. That emotion, inappropriate and unexpected, struck him dumb.

"Travis lives in a trailer," Romy said. "Down by the lake."

"But only until I find a house for us," added Honey, who'd slipped unseen onto the deck and now stood by the door with Nicole.

At the sound of her voice, Travis abandoned Andy and hurried back to his mother. From the back pocket of his jeans, he extracted a plastic billfold—the western-looking kind with lacing around the edges from which he withdrew a piece of paper. "I brought you a note from my teacher."

"Already?" Honey teased, eyes twinkling attractively.

Andy's gut twisted at the sight of mother and child, and the painful stab this time was one he'd come to know well the past year and a half—regret. Regret that he couldn't pick up his own child after school; regret that there wouldn't be impulsive stops at the ice-cream shop; regret that he'd never see the notes from her teachers.

"This is about peewee football." Honey sounded almost horrified.

"Yeah," Travis replied. "I'm going to play."

"But you don't know how," his mother argued.

"Sure I do," Travis insisted, the next moment adding, "practice starts on Thursday. Can I go?"

"Let me think about it, okay?" Honey replied.

"Aw, Mom."

"We'll talk some more tonight," she told him, words that produced a huff of impatience from Travis, but he didn't argue.

Andy couldn't help but notice that neither mentioned a daddy, who just might know something about the sport. He frowned slightly, wondering about it.

"I bet you'd like to finish up here, wouldn't you?" Honey said as though she'd noted and was guessing the reason for Andy's expression. "Come on, kiddos. Let's give Mr. Fulbright some elbow room." She herded the youngsters toward the door and then inside the house, immediately following them herself. Andy heard their voices fading as they walked farther away.

Nicole, still standing on the deck, walked over to him. "So how's it going so far?"

"As expected. I should be assembling the units by the end of the week, first of next week."

"Good." She turned to follow the others indoors.

"Oh, um, Nicole?"

She paused and glanced back at him over her shoulder. "Hmm?"

"Where's Travis's dad? I mean...they didn't mention him at all when they were talking about the football."

"Honey is divorced. Charles, Travis's father, lives back in Boston."

"I see." And he did...all too clearly.

Honey had stolen her child from his father just as his own ex, Jaclyn, had stolen Sarajane.

At once outraged, it was all he could do not to follow Nicole back inside—so he could corner Honey and tell her exactly what he thought of a mother who'd not only deprive her son of the chance to play football, but would cheat that same son's father of the chance to be involved.

Women.

Except for a rare few—Ethan's lady love among them—all women were alike: heartless, conniving, selfish. And though seemingly as sweet as her name, Honey had just proved herself to be no exception to the rule.

Thank goodness he'd found out the truth before his physical attraction to the woman prompted him to do something as stupid as asking her out. Now he'd play it smart, of course.

Any further contact between them would have to be initiated by Honorine and kept as brief as possible by Andy.

Chapter Two

"How do you take your coffee?"

Since these words were Andy Fulbright's first that Tuesday morning, Honey started when he spoke to her from the doorway of the bedroom-turned-workroom, sometime around ten o'clock. She noted that he looked every bit as attractive as he had yesterday—maybe even more so since he held two mugs of coffee.

"Black would be heavenly," she told him.

With a solemn nod, Andy walked over to where she sat on the floor, once again surrounded by books. He handed her one of the steaming mugs from which she immediately drank.

"Mmm, thanks." Wondering why he'd ignored her all morning, Honey gave the carpenter a friendly smile intended to invite conversation. "You really *are* handy in the kitchen...at least with the coffeemaker. How are you with pots, pans and skillets?"

"Have you made a decision?" Andy asked, ignoring her smile, her compliment and her joking question.

Honey frowned slightly into her drink and tried to recall any unsolved, library-type dilemmas they might've discussed the day before.

"About what?"

"Travis's playing peewee football."

"Oh, that." She shook her head and sighed, at once recalling the animated discussion she'd had with her son earlier that morning on that very subject. "I just don't see how he can."

"Why is that?"

"Several reasons," Honey good-naturedly replied. The issue was really none of Andy's concern, after all. "First, I don't know anything about the sport, so I can't help him. Second, he might get hurt, and third, if he stays after school to practice for an hour, he won't have a ride home. Right now, Nicole gets him when she picks up Ethan's kids since I don't finish up here until five o'clock or after."

"Can't your husband take up the slack?"

"My ex-husband, Charles, lives in Boston."

"*Boston?* You mean he gave up his rights to Travis?"

"No..."

"Then why in the hell are the two of you living here?"

Not quite believing her ears or Andy's belligerent tone, Honey slowly lowered the half-empty mug. "Excuse me?"

"You should never have moved Travis so far away from his dad. You're cheating them out of special times together."

Honey stared at him in disbelief, astounded by his rudeness and nerve. "You don't know what you're talking about."

"Believe me, I do."

"You couldn't possibly, so I'll thank you to keep your opinions to yourself." Having said that, she got to her feet, brushed past him, and exited the room in a huff.

"Not hearing the truth won't make it go away," Andy called after her. The next instant, Honey heard the thump of his boots as he followed her down the parquet-floored hall to the kitchen. There he caught her arm and turned her to face him. "Travis and his dad should be going places, doing things. They're missing out, *and it's your fault.*"

Honey angrily jerked her arm free. "Charles Truman *is* missing out, but it's his own fault, not mine. Now I'm not going to discuss this any further with you. Not only do you not know the facts of this matter, they aren't your business, anyway." With that, Honey walked to the sink and poured out the rest of the coffee, which had suddenly lost its flavor.

"What's to know besides the fact that your husband has to travel twelve hundred miles every time he wants to see his son?"

"Charlie is not my husband anymore!" Honey exclaimed, whirling to stand nose-to-chin with Andy. She drew in a calming breath before adding, "He's somebody else's now."

"Is that why you stole his child away? Revenge?"

"Oh, good grief!"

"Well, is it?" Andy glowered at her. "Is it?"

Though tempted to end the conversation by kicking his shin and stalking away, Honey didn't. There was something in Andy's eyes that belied his irrational animosity. She saw pain in their blue depths and wondering at the reason for it, she somehow held on to her patience.

"I didn't steal Travis away. Charlie agreed to the relocation in writing, probably because it relieved him of the responsibility of seeing his son."

"What do you mean?" Andy asked, frowning. He, too, set aside his coffee.

"I mean that even though we lived barely a mile apart, Charlie hadn't made any attempt to see Travis for at least six months before we moved."

Andy's jaw dropped. "What kind of custody rights does this ex of yours have?"

"Legally he has Travis every other week. That became a burden after three months, though, so it's been sporadic visits ever since."

"And you've been divorced how long?"

"Two and a half years... if you must know." She put emphasis on the last phrase to remind him that she really didn't have to share any of this. Why she'd shared it at all, Honey couldn't say. The man had no more right to the details of her private life than he had good manners.

Andy stared at her in silence for a moment, then shook his head and sighed. "Sorry. It's just that—" Abruptly he caught himself, aborting whatever explanation he'd started to make.

"What?" Honey prompted, at once curious.

He didn't speak at first, then shrugged. "As a dad who'd give the world for a chance to spend time with his kid, I can't help but sympathize with the plight of all ex-husbands who are fathers. More often than not, we get a bum rap in court."

So that was it. "You're divorced, too?"

"Three years now."

"And you have a son?"

"A daughter... Sarajane."

"Age?"

"Six."

Very close to her son's age. No wonder Andy couldn't contain his bitterness. "I take it your wife has custody."

"Yes. She and Sarajane live in France with her new husband."

"France..." Honey breathed the word, trying to imagine what it would be like to have a child so far away. "How could you let her go?"

"*I* couldn't. A judge made the decision." Though Andy's blue eyes swam with unshed tears, he didn't look away or otherwise appear embarrassed about his show of emotion. "I get her two months in the summer, plus a few holidays."

Which obviously wasn't enough for him. *Lucky Sarajane,* Honey thought, her heart twisting with regret that Travis's father wasn't capable of such devotion. She'd never have moved from Boston if Charlie had shown that kind of interest in their son.

"I'm very sorry. It's obvious that you're not one of the Charlies of this world, but a father who really loves his child. I know you must miss her terribly."

"I miss her." Andy turned then, walked over to the patio door and slipped outside onto the deck. He picked up his tool belt, but didn't put it on, instead staring at it as though not exactly sure how. Clearly he had much on his mind.

Honey could guess what...and who...so she encouraged him to talk. "Tell mc about your Sarajane. Does she have your dark hair and navy eyes?"

Andy smiled slightly and shook his head. "Nah. She has Jaclyn's blond hair and light, light blue eyes. She's very petite and looks as delicate as a china doll." He gave Honey a full-fledged grin. "But I'll match her against any boy any day...one her age, that is."

"A tomboy?"

"From the get-go."

"Is she into sports?"

"Yes. She played softball the two months I had her this summer. I coached her team."

"So you're a softball coach. No wonder you think I should let Travis get involved in sports."

"Actually, I coach softball in the summer, peewee football in the fall. And for that reason more than any, I know you should let Travis play. The discipline will be good for him. He'll make new friends and learn how to win and how to lose."

"So you're one of the peewee coaches...." She eyed him for a moment, possibilities dancing inside her head. "Would you consider—?"

"Why don't I—?"

They stopped, then laughed together.

"You first," Honey prompted, hoping she knew what he was going to say.

"I was just going to volunteer to help you out on this football thing. I could bring Travis over here after practice. It would be right on my way."

"I'd pay you, of course."

"Of course nothing. I'll probably be dropping off this or that kid, so I don't mind seeing after Travis. As for your not knowing anything about football...don't worry. That's the purpose of coaches, just as the purpose of shoulder pads and helmets is to keep your son from getting hurt."

"Are you sure about this? Travis is liable to drive you crazy. He's starved for adult male attention."

"And I'm starved for kid stuff—the reason I coach in the first place. We'll be good for each other."

Too true, Honey realized, a thought that made her smile. Travis needed a man in his life, even if she didn't. And it appeared as if Andy needed a child in his. Maybe they could work a deal.... "Thanks a million."

"You're very welcome," he murmured, smiling back. Honey noted that his eyes twinkled now, and all traces of pain had vanished. "Travis is going to need some special gear that isn't provided by the team sponsors. I could take him to get it Wednesday night if you like. I can't tonight because I'm tied up."

"Wednesday night would be fine... and thanks. I'm really ignorant of the game."

"That's okay. I'm an expert. Ask me anything you want to know, anything at all."

"Now? Don't you have work to do?" Honey asked, glancing around at the lumber he'd been sawing all morning.

As though suddenly remembering why he stood on the deck, knee-deep in boards, Andy made short work of strapping on his tool belt and reaching for one of them. "So we'll talk at lunch... or do you have other plans?"

"No plans."

"Are you brown-bagging it?"

"Yes, as a matter of fact."

"So am I. What say we meet under that oak tree at high noon?" He pointed to a massive oak that shaded the east side of the house.

"A picnic? I'd love it." She moved toward the door.

"Honey?"

She turned and found him staring at her, cheeks stained crimson.

"I meant Honey with a capital *H*," he quickly explained.

"Of course."

"I'm really sorry I was such a bear this morning. I had no right."

"You had no right, true, but every reason," she told him as she stepped into the kitchen.

At noon, they met as planned. Since there would be no furniture in the library until Wednesday, Honey flattened two of the cardboard boxes she'd emptied so they could sit on them, protecting their clothes from the grass.

As they ate, they talked about peewee football... or Andy did, anyway. Honey simply listened and tried to absorb the information which ranged from how late the season started and how long it lasted, thanks to the mild southern climate, to the purpose and instruction in the basics of the sport.

According to Andy, the coaches were actually allowed on the playing field to place the boys, shout out directions and encouragement, and explain the referee's calls. Any boy could join up. The goal of each team was learning, not winning.

Honey, nibbling a ham sandwich, registered most of Andy's lecture and approved his philosophy. Not a sports enthusiast, however, she found part of her attention naturally straying to more important things—his flashing eyes, his dimples, the rugged line of his jaw and chin.

She also noted and approved his slightly receding hairline and his muscled neck and shoulders. Bulging biceps commanded her attention, too, as did his forearms and his legs, obviously well built, undoubtedly strong.

Clearly the man was used to hard labor, and Honey couldn't help but respond to the highly evident physical fruits of it. She found herself picturing how he'd look in a bathing suit or, better yet, in nothing at all, these visions making her squirm.

"You look a little flushed. Are you too warm?"

More like too hot, Honey silently answered Andy's question. But she did nothing more than shake her head in response, of course. It would never do to admit that the mere sight of him awakened hormones long slumbering. Long slumbering? Or slumbering too long? she immediately wondered, a question wisely filed away for future consideration. Sitting *this* close to *this* man was no time to wonder about the state of her libido. Such thoughts were dangerous to unattached women who intended to remain that way—especially one as hot-blooded as she.

"On second thought, it is rather warm, isn't it?" Abruptly Honey got to her feet and smoothed her jeans and shirt. "But that's okay. Lunch hour is over according to my watch."

"So it is." Andy scrambled to his feet and made short work of cleaning up the evidence of their picnic. Together they walked the short distance to the deck-turned-carpentry-shop. "Any lunch plans for tomorrow?"

"Not really."

"Then why don't I demonstrate just how good I am with pots, pans and skillet? Lunch . . . my treat."

"I was just kidding you this morning," Honey hastily explained. "You seemed so cool compared to yesterday. I wanted to break the ice."

"And instead, I dumped it over your head . . . figuratively speaking, of course." He shook his head, clearly regretful. "Come on, Honey. I owe you lunch at least, for being such a jerk."

"Then by all means, pay up," she replied even as her common sense whispered, *Honey, we need to talk.*

"Shall we rendezvous under our oak at twelve hundred hours?"

Rendezvous? *Our* oak?

"Why not?" Honey replied. And though a hundred and one very good answers to that question sprang to mind at once, she ignored them all.

The moment Honey arrived at the library on Wednesday, she got to work supervising the men Nicole had hired to move office furniture salvaged from the Winter mansion. With little more than a nod of greeting to Andy, hard at work on the deck out back, she then passed the rest of the morning setting up her office. That chore involved arranging the furnishings and emptying her station wagon of numerous professional items of her own—computer and printer, reference books, office supplies—stashed in boxes there.

So involved was she in her task that she actually forgot their lunch date until she smelled something spicy. Honey soon followed her nose to the kitchen, where she found Andy standing before the stove, stirring a skillet full of what looked to be some sort of hamburger-tomato-noodle dish that had probably originated in a box.

Pausing at the door to the combination kitchen-dining room, Honey took note of four bar stools, which hadn't been there yesterday, as well as a couch, a recliner, a coffee table and a television.

"Where did these come from?" she exclaimed, as she walked into the room, turning slowly around to take in the transformation from dining room to employee lounge.

Andy shrugged. "A delivery about a half hour ago from the big house. Since I was in here already, I helped unload."

"Why didn't you yell out for me?" Honey asked, now walking over to sniff the savory steam emanating from the bubbling contents of the skillet.

"Actually, I did," Andy replied. "When you didn't come, I just handled it."

"I'm sorry. I do have a one-track mind, and I was busy hooking up my computer, I guess."

Andy grinned. "No problem. Ready to eat?"

"Mmm-hmm."

"We have a place to sit now." He motioned toward the breakfast bar, now functional thanks to the addition of the four tall stools. Honey noticed that he'd set out paper plates and plastic forks. "I'm into disposable," he explained, obviously following her gaze.

"So am I." Seating herself on one of the stools, Honey watched while Andy spooned out a liberal helping of his concoction.

"I try to stay away from salt, so I didn't use any. Feel free to add some if you need to," he said, handing her the plate.

"Is it iodized?"

"Excuse me?"

"The salt. Is it iodized?"

"Why do you ask?"

"I'm allergic to iodine."

"Yeah?" He picked up the blue cardboard cylinder and read the label. "'Iodized salt.' Sorry about that."

"Probably won't need it, anyway." She waited until he'd served himself and sat beside her before sampling the dish. "Why, this is wonderful! And perfectly seasoned, I might add."

"You sound surprised." *He* sounded amused.

"I have to admit that I am. I figured this was one of those prepackaged casserole helpers."

"Nope. My ex-mother-in-law gave me the recipe."

"No kidding." She took another mouthful and savored the taste. "Have you always cooked or is this a postdivorce phenomenon?"

Andy considered her question a moment. "Pre and post, really. The last two years we were married, Jaclyn was on location a lot. I became chief cook and bottle washer... literally."

"What do you mean 'on location'? Is your wife a movie star or something?"

"No, she's a hairdresser...a talented, much-respected, highly overpaid hairdresser to the stars." He got up and poured himself another glass of the sun tea he'd apparently brought for their lunch.

Honey raised her glass for a refill, which he gave her. "Do I detect a note of bitterness?"

"Let's just say the two of us got along better when she did hair at the Cinderella Shop...not that I begrudge her an exciting career in the movies. I didn't and don't. I just wish—" Abruptly he halted. "But let's not talk about my marital woes. Let's talk about yours." He grinned. "What does Charlie—it was Charlie, wasn't it?—do for a living?"

"He's president of Truman Shipping," Honey told him. "A position given to him as a wedding present by his mother when he remarried last year to the *right* woman."

"Do I detect a note of bitterness?" Andy asked, exactly mimicking her earlier question.

"Let's just say we got along better before his father and mother talked him into moving back home—after a grand total of six months of wedded bliss."

"Home as in Boston?"

"Home as in the family mansion."

"Ah. Two families under one roof. That can be stressful. . . ."

"Terminally so," Honey murmured, instantly recalling the numerous times that she and Charlie's overly possessive mother had butted heads over him.

Andy's eyes, shining with curiosity, invited her to share the juicy details.

"Do you get along with your in-laws?" she asked, instead of cooperating.

"Oh, yeah. They were not happy when Jaclyn remarried and moved to France. Jaclyn's their only child, after all, and Sarajane is their only grandchild."

"A close family?"

"Very. Jaclyn and Sarajane fly in at least once every three or four months to see them."

"And they live where?"

"Right here in Winterhaven."

Honey thought about that for a moment, then smiled. "Ah. The reason you decided to move back."

"You've got it. They call me whenever Sarajane's in town."

"Clever man."

Andy shook his head. "No. A clever man would never marry for love."

"So you did that, too, huh?"

"Yes, but it won't ever be a prerequisite again."

Honey had to nod her agreement with his sentiment. "There are several musts that are higher on my list, too."

"Such as?"

"Well, for one, I—"

"Yo, Andy!"

Honey turned at the sound of that jovial greeting and saw that a tall blond man now stood at the door leading to the living room.

"Hi, Jack," Andy said, motioning for the man to join them. He turned to Honey. "This is Jack Austin, the partner you haven't met. Jack, Honorine Truman, Winterhaven's new librarian."

"Librarian, you say?" Slowly, a look of surprise on his face, Jack walked into the room, right hand extended. "Nice to meet you." He shook her hand, released it, and then turned to Andy. "If they'd made 'em like this when I was in school, I'd probably have my Ph.D."

Though undoubtedly sexist, the words did not offend Honey, who'd often heard such comments. Instead she just laughed at this partner and friend of Andy and Ethan. He had a nice smile, she decided, and was easy on the eyes, if not as ruggedly handsome as Andy.

"What's cooking?" He'd turned his attention to their plates, a sure indication he was as comfortable with her as she was with him. He walked to the stove and sniffed at Andy's creation, still bubbling gently. "Is this some of Wanda's goulash?"

"Yes," Andy told him.

"Hot damn!" he said, reaching for the package of paper plates. Belatedly he froze and glanced back at Andy. "She really made a lot... I mean, there's enough for me to have one small plate, isn't there?"

"I'm the cook," Andy replied. "And yes, there's enough to share."

"*You* made this?" Jack arched an eyebrow in obvious surprise. "I thought you hated cooking this stuff."

Honey turned to Andy in surprise. "You hate to cook this?"

Andy, clearly embarrassed, glared at Jack before shifting his attention to Honey. "The recipe is sort of complicated," he explained, "so I save it for special occasions."

"What's special about today?" Jack asked, his mouth now full of the savory goulash. He ate standing, plate in one hand, fork in the other.

Andy, visibly at a loss, hesitated before speaking. "Getting started on this library project, I guess. That's certainly cause for celebration. Right, Honey?"

Jack instantly had a coughing spasm. Red-faced and sputtering, he set down his plate and reached for one of the coffee mugs drying in a dish rack next to the sink. He filled it with tap water, then drank several swallows.

Concerned, Honey joined him at the sink and patted him on the back in much the same way as she patted Travis when he choked on some food. "Are you okay?"

"Yeah," he replied, his voice a little the worse for wear. His expression unreadable, Jack looked from Honey to Andy and back to Honey. She noted his frown and the speculation in his eyes and wondered at it.

"Honey is Honorine's nickname," Andy said then, his words explaining Jack's confusion and making her laugh.

"Oh." He laughed, too. "For a minute there, I thought..." He laughed again and shook his head. "This business with Ethan and Nicole has really spooked me."

"What business?" Honey asked, thinking she'd missed something.

"This wedding." Jack began to eat again, this time more slowly. "When the three of us first moved to Winterhaven back in May, we swore to each other that we'd stay free and clear of women for six months."

"Good grief, why?" she couldn't help but ask.

"So we could concentrate on making a go of Do It Right, Inc.," Andy replied. "We had a rocky start...well, maybe it was slower than it was rocky...and we thought it'd be better if we all paid attention to what we were doing instead of worrying about some Jane, er, woman."

Jack nodded. "Two months later, Ethan approached Nicole about renovating her dad's house. One second after that, he fell for her."

Honey bit back her laugh at his horrified expression. "He went back on his word, huh?"

"That's right." Jack refilled his plate from the ample supply of goulash. "Any salt around here? You never add enough."

Andy handed Jack the box, then exchanged an amused glance with Honey.

"So are you and Andy still bound by the promise?" She asked the question of Jack, but her gaze stayed on Andy.

"No," the dark-haired carpenter replied before his partner could.

Jack, his fork hovering halfway between mouth and plate, looked from one to the other of them again.

"No?" Honey's gaze locked with Andy's.

"No."

"Oh."

For long seconds, they assessed each other. She saw in him the kind of man her mother had wished for her: gainfully employed. She also saw the kind of man she'd once wished for herself: handsome.

But that was then. Now, older and wiser, she'd seek other qualities if she was looking—qualities such as loyalty and kindness, love of children, and honesty. If she was looking...

Which she wasn't.

Jack cleared his throat, a sound that drew the attention of both Honey and Andy since he'd been choking only moments before. "Guess I'll be going," he muttered, edging for the door, plate and plastic fork in hand.

"Did you stop by for a reason?" Andy asked, his question halting Jack midstride.

"Oh, yeah, I did. Are you still coming over tonight to help me put that entertainment center together?"

"I'll be there."

"Good." He walked to the door, but stopped again and turned back to Andy. "Bring the rest of the goulash, okay?"

"I'll bring it."

With a goodbye nod to Honey, Jack disappeared into the living room. Moments later, they heard the screen door slam behind him.

"So what do you think of Jack?" Andy asked Honey without hesitation.

"He seems nice enough," she answered.

"Nice? I was expecting handsome or sexy."

"I guess some women might find him desirable." Honey walked back to the bar and sat next to Andy again, her body turned slightly toward him, her heels resting on the lower rung of the stool. "He's not my type, though."

"What is your type?" He, too, turned, a move that put them knee-to-knee and elbow-to-elbow.

At once, Honey's heart began to thud against her rib cage. "I'm, er, not really sure," she stammered, the next instant adding, "and it doesn't matter, anyway. I'm not in the market for a guy."

"You're not?"

"No."

"Well, I'm not in the market for a gal, either."

"You're not?"

"No." Their gazes locked. He swayed toward her almost imperceptibly, but enough to quicken her thudding heartbeat to an almost painful pace.

"It's because we've both learned our lessons," she said. "We both know better."

"Yes," he agreed. "We know better, but sometimes... sometimes we still want."

Honey, drowning in a sudden wave of just that want, had to close her eyes for just a moment to block out the sight of his mouth, so kissably close. So damned kissably close. "We're only human, Andy," she said with a sigh. "We've both loved and been loved. It's only natural that we might be tempted now and then."

"Only natural," he echoed.

"But we're too smart to give in to it."

"Much too smart," he said.

And then he kissed her.

Chapter Three

It was a zinger of a kiss—the toe-curling kind capable of turning a levelheaded single mom into a simpering ninny.

Honey allowed herself one whole minute of it before she placed a hand on Andy's chest and pushed him away. Lips still tingling from the incredible caress, she drew in a shaky breath and asked, "Why'd you do that?"

"That has been on my mind ever since we met. I got it over with to clear the air so I could concentrate on building the shelves."

So he'd felt it, too—the attraction, the spark between them. And now, curiosity satisfied, he could forget it.

"As kisses go, this one *wasn't* particularly exciting, was it?" she therefore commented. A lie. As kisses went, this one rated six on a scale of one to five—not bad for sixty seconds' contact.

He sat back, eyeing her with visible surprise. "I could do better."

"I'm sure you could," she calmly replied, slipping off the stool and gathering up the paper plates. "And so could I, if I wanted to. I don't, however, nor do you. Besides that, I'm supposed to be working from 8:00 a.m. until 5:00 p.m. I don't have time to waste experimenting with you."

"So Nicole pays you by the hour?"

"By the month, actually, but I maintain a strict work schedule. It's the only way I can be productive."

"She pays me by the job."

"Well, whether we're getting paid by the month or by the job, we both have more important things to do than fool around this way. It's not as if this will take us anywhere. We're both happy just as we are—blissfully unattached—at least romantically. So why don't you run along now? I'll clean up the kitchen."

Run along, huh? Translating that to the "get lost" it certainly was—Honorine was an expert at abrupt dismissals—Andy left her there after pointing out the plastic dish he'd brought along to store leftovers in.

Once outside again, he put his mind on his work, only now and then thinking of their brief but amazingly potent kiss.

He couldn't believe she'd thought it unexciting. What was the woman used to, for Pete's sake? His own mouth was still in shock from the contact. He found himself wishing they could try the kiss again, this time deepening it so he could really sample the flavor that was Honey. For that matter, he wished they could do more than just kiss, since there were other parts of her he anxiously wanted to sample.

But no. Not only had she made it plain that she wasn't interested in more than kissing—and actually not even in that—such experimentation could prove dangerous to a single man such as he. His long-neglected libido was a virtual Pandora's box, just waiting to be opened so it could wreak havoc on his precarious peace of mind and body. Their lunch kiss was something like the fitting of her key into his lock—a reverse sexual metaphor that made him grin in spite of his bad mood.

Obviously if they didn't kiss a second time—if Honey didn't turn the key—no more harm could be done. Though admittedly still tempted to try that second kiss, Andy didn't worry very long that he'd ever give in and do it. It took two to experiment, and if Honey's cool response to their first try was any indication at all, there would be no further testing.

Though Jack asked several leading questions that night while the two of them put together his new entertainment center, Andy didn't share any of what had transpired between him and Honey or how he felt about it. He did reassure Jack that he would lose no sleep over Madam Librarian and was then reassured, in turn, that Jack wouldn't, either.

Andy could only hope *Jack* meant what he said. As for himself, Andy actually lay awake most of that night, hugging a pillow and wishing it were one Honey of a woman.

On Wednesday, Andy barely saw or spoke to the librarian, but only because she didn't arrive at the library until well after lunch. She had in her arms a box—library supplies, she said, bought in Birmingham that morning.

Honorine made several trips back to her car, steadfastly refusing all the offers of help he called out to her from the deck, then spent the rest of the afternoon in her office. Disgustingly disappointed that today found her so preoccupied, Andy had to content himself with nothing more than a peek at her when he came indoors to the bathroom.

Around four o'clock, the banging of the front door announced the arrival of Travis, this time alone. Guessing that Nicole had just dropped him off, Andy called out a greeting. In a heartbeat, Travis stood beside him on the deck, taking in every detail of Andy's work area with a typical little boy's curiosity and enthusiasm.

"Getting excited about football?" Andy asked, highly conscious of Travis's admiring gaze.

"Yes, sir." Unlike his mother, who must have had Southern roots, the boy's accent was Boston all the way, and Andy wondered briefly if the other kids teased him about it. Travis, small of stature, was the sort of kid a bully loved.

"We'll go tonight to get your shoes and stuff."

"Yes, sir." So quiet, so polite. Almost unnaturally so. Who could take credit for that? Andy wondered. Honey? Her ex? "Can I help you measure that board?"

"I don't know. Can you?"

Travis nodded eagerly.

Without a word, Andy handed Travis the metal tape measure. While Andy held one end secure, Travis walked the length of the board, extending the tape to the required distance. Andy handed him a pencil, with which he meticulously marked the wood.

"Now can I help you saw?"

Andy had to think about that. "A saw's very dangerous. But I will let you turn it on for me."

Travis nodded his agreement with the terms.

After retrieving extra safety goggles and positioning them on Travis's face, Andy picked up the board and led the child to the table saw. There, he allowed Travis to flip the power switch on, as promised, and then off again when he finished cutting. Travis next helped by carrying the smaller of the two pieces back to the worktable.

"And what is this?"

At the sound of his mother's voice, Travis turned and grinned. "I'm helping Andy."

"Mr. Fulbright," Honey immediately corrected.

"Call me Coach," Andy said, adding, "Travis is a good hand. Maybe he'll grow up to be a carpenter."

"Would you like to build things?" Honey asked her son, now seated on the deck playing with some lumber scraps.

"Uh-huh," Travis told her. "A house."

Honey laughed. "We do need one, don't we?" She turned to Andy. "Our trailer is so small. I can't wait to find something bigger."

"You've been looking?"

"For weeks, actually. Nicole sent me real estate ads for a whole month before I actually moved here, but there just wasn't anything suitable. Now most of my stuff is in storage, and I sure miss it."

"I could build you a house." The words tumbled off Andy's lips before he could stop them. "I'd have to finish up here first, of course."

"That's very kind," Honey replied, tugging her son to his feet and brushing the sawdust off his jeans. "But I have to have something that's furnished, and I doubt that I could afford you, anyway."

"I'm sure we could work a deal...." Though Andy meant nothing by the offer—his tongue was still on autopilot—Honey tensed visibly and ushered Travis to the door.

"Your snack is on the bar," she said, giving the boy a little push to get him going in that direction. When he disappeared inside, she walked back to Andy. "And just what kind of deal are we talking here?" she asked, her voice low enough so that little ears couldn't hear it.

"Obviously not the kind of deal you've got in mind," Andy replied, adding, "I only meant that my fee is always negotiable. I'm not averse to helping out a single mom."

"I don't take charity."

"And I seldom give it."

"So we're back to what you'd expect in return for your labors...." She positively glared at him, an overreaction he found baffling.

"I'd expect cash on completion, just like any other carpenter. What's your problem, Honey Truman? What have I said to tick you off?"

She stared at him for a moment longer, then sighed. "I'm sorry. I guess I'm a little touchy today."

"Yeah? Why?"

"That kiss yesterday... the one you forgot as soon as it happened..."

She thought he'd forgotten the kiss that easily? "What about the kiss?"

"I couldn't sleep last night for thinking about it."

"I kept you up?"

"Yes." Stepping closer, she framed his face with her hands. "And what I have to know is did I keep you up?"

Andy exhaled slowly through his teeth. "Literally, actually."

It took a moment for his answer to sink in, another for the unfortunate wording of her question to register. Immediately her face blushed as pink as the roses planted all around the deck. "I can't believe I said that," she groaned, releasing him and turning away.

"I'm glad you did," Andy replied. "It gets this thing out in the open, er, this attraction I mean." Now *he* was the flustered one.

Honey bubbled with laughter. "I'm glad we've had this discussion. I feel better now." That said, she turned on her heel and started inside.

Eyes rounded in disbelief, Andy caught up with her in two strides. Ever conscious of Travis, now watching cartoons on the television in the dining room, mere feet away, Andy tugged her into a far corner of the deck.

"You may feel better," he told Honey, "but I sure as hell don't."

"You don't?" She leaned against the rail and gazed up at him, clearly surprised.

"No. Honesty may be the best policy, but it can create problems of its own."

"What do you mean?"

"I mean it can raise some interesting questions." He stepped closer.

She gulped audibly and would have stepped back if the rail hadn't stopped her. "Such as . . . ?"

"Where do we go from here?"

Honey put out a hand, holding him at arm's length. "I was afraid that's what you were going to ask."

"And the answer is . . . ?"

"Let me think for a minute." She turned her back on him and looked out over the lawn. Andy did what came naturally, moving one step closer so that he stood just behind her, their bodies brushing lightly, his hands covering hers on the rail.

He intended to do nothing more than that, but in seconds the scent of her assailed him—a tantalizing blend of baby shampoo, roses and a spicy something he couldn't immediately identify. It was that mystery aroma that most likely got the better of him. At any rate, he nuzzled her hair with his face.

Honey tensed, and Andy could have sworn she whispered, "Please..."

Did she beg him to stop...or continue?

After a quick glance over his shoulder to see if they had a witness, Andy proceeded to find out by touching his lips to the spot of flesh just below her earlobe—flesh readily accessible since she was wearing her hair twisted up into a knot. Honey gasped and jerked her head away, then freed her hands from his and turned, not an easy accomplishment since Andy's body pressed hers into the railing and virtually prevented movement.

Now standing face-to-face with him, she gazed into his eyes. "No, Andy."

"No?"

"No."

Well, hell! He stepped back to let her pass, but to his surprise, she didn't move.

"It's been such a long time since I...since a man..."

"And I'm rushing you, aren't I?" Andy asked, instantly guessing where she was headed. "We'll slow down."

She laughed softly, a sound bereft of humor. "You don't understand, Andy. I don't want to slow down. I want to speed up. I've suddenly remembered how...how—" she struggled visibly for just the right word "—explosive it can be between a man and a woman, and I'm dying to experience the excitement, the danger, the power again."

Hot damn! "Your place or mine?"

"Neither, Andy."

"But you just said—"

"I said what I wanted, not what I can have. Seldom are the two compatible. You must know that."

Andy did know that.

"I have an impressionable son and a demanding job. I can't afford the luxury of sexual involvement with a man—assuming you really do want me that way." She hesitated as though suddenly unsure of herself.

"I want you," Andy replied, and knew it was true.

An astonishing discovery, that. Andy's knees threatened to buckle as the ramifications immediately began to register. An affair. A woman—*this woman*—in his bed. Or Andy in hers. Hurried trysts. Pretending to be strangers when, in truth, they were lovers.

That they would have to pretend, Andy didn't doubt for a moment. Parenthood, small-town respectability and Southern morality demanded it.

"And you understand why we can't have an affair?" Honey asked, gently drawing him back to the reality of their situation.

"Yes." And it certainly wasn't for the same reason she believed they couldn't. In spite of all his recent protestations to the contrary—in particular to Jack—he was a marrying man and incapable of today's casual affairs.

"Good." She smiled at him. "Isn't it amazing how much we understand each other? I mean, we're practically strangers, yet you already know me well enough to see that I'd be useless to Travis and Nicole if we hooked up."

"Useless," Andy agreed, though he could only guess what she really meant.

"I've always been like that," Honey continued, oblivious to the fact that Andy didn't quite get her drift. "Why, in no time I'd be cooking for you, washing for you, cleaning for you—anything to wangle your full commitment and a proposal that neither of us wants." She sighed. "I'm cursed with traditional roots—a nest builder to the nth degree—and that's why it's better that we just play this thing safe and maintain a strict code of conduct."

Her spiel apparently complete, Honey touched his face, then slipped past and joined her son indoors.

Andy turned slowly and stared after her, one hand on the railing for support, the other pressed to his churning gut. So she was the marrying kind, too, and after making as many claims to the contrary as he had. Who'd have guessed?

Not Andy, now fully aware of just how dangerous Honorine Truman really was and, therefore, soaked in a nervous sweat resulting from his close call with disaster.

She was right. A strict code of conduct was definitely in order and once clarified, should be adhered to with a vengeance by both of them.

"I smell toast," Travis announced to his mom the moment he and Andy burst into her trailer that night around seven. Judging from the number of packages they carried, their shopping trip had undoubtedly been a success.

"You smell cinnamon," Honey told him and held up a stick of the spice.

"So that's the mystery smell!" Andy exclaimed, a cryptic remark if Honey ever heard one.

"What?"

"Nothing," he replied instead of explaining. "What's that you're doing with the cinnamon?"

"I'm tying it on these Christmas wreaths I'm making for the elementary school." She smiled at Andy. "Have you heard of their November Nights festival? It's on Saturday—a money-making project. I've already been roped into helping out."

"Some of my football players told me about it. The festival is really a lot of fun, according to them."

"Yeah," Travis eagerly agreed, his dark eyes glowing with excitement. "They have a hayride and a fishing thing where you get prizes and a place where you throw pies at the teachers and everything. Me and Mom are going to have a great time."

Honey, who knew her son would have to spend most of his festival time at her side since she'd been talked into running the handicraft room, didn't respond to that. Later would be soon enough to tell him she wouldn't be able to accompany him to the various activities.

Andy grinned at Travis, then eyed the colorful calico scraps lying all over the tiny kitchen table, along with a portable sewing machine, candy canes, lollipops, ribbons and all sorts of other trim. Suspended from a clothes hanger were a couple of the wreaths she'd completed that evening. "These are really nice."

"You think?" Honey rose and walked over to join him, where she perused her handiwork with a critical eye. "I found a pattern in a magazine and it looked simple and Christmasy."

"They're perfect," he assured her. "So perfect that I'll buy one for my front door."

"You want one?" Impulsively she reached out and handed a wreath to him. "For your time tonight."

"This is much too much payment for tonight. Travis and I had a good time, didn't we, sport?"

Travis nodded. "We got everything I need."

"Oh?" Honey took their packages, set them on a chair and began to pilfer through them. She pulled out socks, shoes, a pair of spandex shorts and a few other items not so readily identified. "What are the shorts for? I thought they wore pants with pads in them."

"The shorts go under the pants," Andy replied.

"Why?"

"Skin protection, and—" he winked at Travis "—they might come in handy if he splits his pants."

"I see." Honey next held up a flat box and read, "Athletic supporter, size S. What's this?"

"Mo-om!" Travis groaned the word in two syllables, a sure indication she'd embarrassed him.

Andy just laughed. "I take it you've never been around male athletes."

"No." Charlie's most strenuous exercise had been braking his Ferrari. Her dad's, mowing the lawn. She had no brothers.

"It's something they wear to protect their, um—"

"Privates," Travis interjected.

"Exactly." Andy grinned at the boy.

Thoroughly disconcerted, Honey dropped the offending object back into the box, then handed it to her son. "Take it." He did. She turned to Andy.

"Did I give you enough money?"

"No, you owe me five dollars and thirty-one cents."

With a nod, Honey dug the money out of her billfold and handed it to him. "Thanks. I really appreciate this."

"No problem." He moved toward the door, only to pause before leaving. "Travis, You know I'm giving you a ride home after practice?" Travis nodded. "Then I guess I'll see you two tomorrow."

"You aren't staying for dinner, Coach?" Travis's eyes, round and pleading, were as painful to Honey as a knife stab to the heart. Obviously he already adored Andy, and no wonder. There was much to admire about the man—his generosity, his humor, his kindness.

"You can, you know," she said. "We're just having hot dogs, and there's more than enough."

"Oh, I—"

"Pleeeease? I want to show you my baseball cards."

"You have baseball cards?" Andy asked.

"Yes," Honey answered for her son. "On the floor, on the bed, on the dresser. He just started collecting them and doesn't really know what he's doing."

"Then by all means I'll stay for a hot dog," Andy said. "I've been collecting baseball cards for years, and I have a system that I'll be glad to explain."

Beaming, Travis took Andy's hand and led him down the short hallway to his room. Honey didn't follow, instead walking over to retrieve hot dogs and mustard from the refrigerator. She knew what she'd have seen if she had followed, though—Andy and Travis in a cramped, cluttered bedroom.

Andy, tall and large, would dominate the room but then, he'd dominate any room. He had that kind of presence. Why, even the kitchen felt different because he'd been there. It was almost a tangible thing, that all-male aura of his and it lit up her little trailer like summer sunshine.

Unthinking, Honey stole a moment to bask in the glow. How she missed having a man around. From a very early age, she'd wanted nothing more than to be a loving wife and devoted mother. That's all. Too bad Fate had other plans.

Fate? Honey sighed. She had only herself to blame for the mess her life was in now. Her own bad decisions were the culprit—her decisions and, perhaps, Charlie's immaturity. But that was water under the bridge, and she'd long since dried the tears that kept it flowing.

A little depressed nonetheless, Honey methodically searched out and found corn chips, a can of chili and the buns. Quickly she heated what needed to be heated, during which time she cleared the table by piling everything onto the couch only a few feet away.

Not for the first time frustrated by their living conditions, Honey snatched up the *Winterhaven Daily* and in seconds scanned the sparse want ads. She found, of all things, a new real estate ad for a furnished three-bedroom home in the heart of town. Without hesitation, Honey dialed the number listed and made an appointment to see it Friday evening after work.

"You've found a house?" Andy asked, walking into the room just as she hung up the phone. On his heels trailed Travis, all smiles and looking happier than he had in weeks.

"I hope so," Honey said. "Now, are you guys hungry?"

"Starved," they chorused and then laughed at the coincidence.

"Good, 'cause dinner is served."

Andy ate two hot dogs. Honey and Travis each ate one—served on paper plates. She gave them ice cream for dessert and then, while Travis bathed, let Andy help her do what little cleaning up had to be done in the kitchen.

"I guess I'd better go," Andy said when they'd finished.

"Would you just stick your head in the bathroom and tell Travis goodbye first? He'll be disappointed if you don't."

"Oh, I was going to." Andy headed down the hall to the bathroom, and Honey heard him say, "Gotta go. See you tomorrow, sport."

"You can't stay and tuck me in?"

Honey, who wouldn't have minded being tucked in by Andy, herself, hurried over to join them. "No, he can't stay to tuck you in. Give the man a break, Travis. He's donated lots of his time to us tonight. He probably has things of his own to do."

Travis, barely visible in a flotilla of bubbles and boats, looked up at Andy. "You have stuff to do?"

"Yeah, but I promise I'll tuck you in next time, okay?"

Next time? There'd be a next time? Honey couldn't hold back her smile. "Now tell Andy goodbye."

"Bye, Coach."

"Bye yourself." Andy turned and slipped past Honey, then walked down the hall and to the door. She joined him there a brief second later and turned on the porch light. "Dinner was nice. Thanks."

"You're welcome. And thank you for helping out tonight."

He nodded, smiled and stepped outside. Honey heard the crunch of gravel beneath his boots as he walked beyond the circle of light to his truck. Just as he opened the door of the vehicle, she remembered the wreath.

"Andy, wait!"

He did, and grinned when she joined him outside, calico craft in hand. "I forgot it."

"You did."

"Thanks."

"My pleasure."

He hesitated, kicked at a rock, then exclaimed, "Oh, what the hell," and reached out to pull her close. "Just one quick one," he promised, adding, "no tongues."

"Well, darn," Honey blurted, thoughtless words that earned her a groan and a kiss that involved lips, teeth and tongues, not to mention other critical body parts.

Held close to him as she was by his arm and the Christmas wreath, Honey actually shared Andy's shiver and heard the hammering of his heart. But apparently that wasn't close enough for him. Without breaking the kiss, he backed them up a step, set the wreath on the front seat of his truck, and then hugged her even tighter by slipping his hands into the back pockets of her jeans and holding her just where she wanted.

There was no mistaking his desire for her. All the physical evidence was there . . . all of it.

And at that realization, Honey, too, shivered.

"Mom?" It was Travis and he sounded damned close.

With a gasp, Honey twisted free and whirled to face the door of the trailer. But her son wasn't silhouetted there. Only belatedly did she remember that the bathroom window was on this side of the mobile home and too high for Travis to look through . . . thank goodness.

"What do you need?" she called back to her son.

"My tugboat."

"It's in the net." Travis had a nylon net full of boats hanging by suction cups on the wall within easy reach.

"I found it!"

Turning her attention back to Andy, who didn't look any better off nervewise than she, Honey shook her head and a finger at him. "You said no tongues."

"You didn't like it?"

"I loved it." Honey huffed her exasperation. "Which just proves that it's not what either of us needs right now."

"True."

"I'm already losing sleep."

"Me, too."

"Why did we ever start this?" she fumed. "I knew better." In utter frustration, Honey tilted her head back and stared at the night sky, black as ink and studded with stars. "Maybe I'll go to the doctor first free minute I find and tell him I need something to put my hormones under control."

Andy laughed at her absurdity. "There's another, less expensive solution."

"I'd like to hear it."

"Sleep with me."

Honey glared at him. "You call that inexpensive? Don't you know what that kind of foolishness might cost us in peace of mind?"

"Yeah, but we'd have peace of body, something I could sure use right now."

"And so could I, but that doesn't make sleeping together any kind of solution." She slumped against the truck door. "Oh, Andy, I'm so sorry."

"Sorry?"

"Yes. Sorry we met, sorry that we kissed, and sorry that my son and I like you so much."

"Well, I'm not," Andy said, a reply that surprised her. "I'm happier than I've been since Sarajane flew back to France. And if sexual frustration is the cost of keeping you and Travis around, then that's the price I'll pay."

Touched by his honesty, Honey blinked back tears. "Travis, you okay in there?" she called out, even as her gaze locked with Andy's.

"Yeah," her son yelled back.

Honey registered the reply with a nod, then stepped up to give the carpenter a hug. He returned it at once, an action she cherished.

"You can relax, Coach. Travis and I are going to be around for a good long while."

"Is that a threat?" His words lightly teased, but Honey felt his tension and saw the slight frown knitting his brow.

"No, it's a promise," she whispered, an answer straight from the heart that earned her Andy's smile, brighter than the rising moon, potent as a love potion, addicting as any drug.

Chapter Four

"Did you have fun today?" Andy asked Travis after Thursday afternoon practice. They walked together from the school yard to the nearby parking lot where Andy's midnight blue truck waited. Colorful autumn leaves crunched beneath their feet with every step.

"Uh-huh," the boy responded, his breath creating a puff of fog in the chilly air. Andy noted that he seemed a bit distracted, almost worried about something. He couldn't imagine what, since there was no doubt in his mind that Travis had enjoyed every minute of football practice. He hadn't even cried when his hand got caught between two players' helmets....

"How's the hand?" Andy asked, suddenly wondering if it was hurt worse than he thought.

Travis held up his left hand to solemnly examine a scrape on the palm, his first football injury. "It stings a little."

"Guess we'd better get your mom to put some antiseptic on it." Andy unlocked the door of the truck so Travis could get in.

"Do we have to?" the child asked, scrambling up onto the vinyl seat. He frowned at the reddened skin, clearly in a quandary. "She might not let me play anymore."

So that was it. Biting back a smile, Andy walked around the truck to the driver's side and slid behind the wheel. "I doubt she'd go that far." Andy reached out to ruffle Travis's dark hair. "But I see your point. Moms do worry a lot."

"Yeah," Travis agreed with a heavy sigh that further threatened Andy's solemn countenance.

"So why don't we stop by my place and take care of the hand before we go to the library?"

Travis brightened immediately. "Yeah!"

Grinning, Andy drove straight to his own house via a route that didn't take them past the Winter place. In his kitchen, the two of them made short work of doctoring Travis's hand with no-sting antiseptic and the fluorescent dinosaur bandages left over from Sarajane's summer visit.

Andy marveled at the change in his kitchen now that the boy stood there. It actually felt . . . warmer . . . almost as if bright sunshine was streaming through the windows. And the sound of Travis's laughter was as melodious as wind chimes dancing in a breeze. Andy felt his spirits lift, and by the time they got back in the truck and drove to the library, Travis was not the only one whose hurt had received first aid.

Honey met them at the door with a smile for both and a "thank you, goodbye" for Andy that was a bit of a letdown. Walking to his truck moments later, he mused that she still seemed as ill at ease with him as she had all day. Could that mean she'd had second thoughts about last night's candid talk and their hot, hot kisses?

Andy was way past second thoughts himself, having stewed over Honey most of last night and every moment today. And the heck of it was he still didn't know exactly what to do about his desire for her. How easy to say he could tolerate sexual frustration to keep her and Travis around. How difficult to actually do it.

But he would, because deep inside he feared getting involved with Honey in that way. Better to play smart with his heart and lurk on the fringes of her world, waiting for whatever crumbs of love and laughter she and her son happened to toss his way.

Andy's house, always too quiet, was a tomb when he entered it that night, thanks to the fact that Travis had been there and gone. Andy paused just inside the door and considered the newly remodeled living room. While it looked picture perfect and should have been cozy, he still hated to come home at night. That feeling told him it was those crumbs of love and laughter—not fresh paint and a new carpet—that his old house needed most to turn it into a home.

Andy focused his gaze on a pile of stones lying on a drop sheet in front of his half-built fireplace. He knew he should devote a few hours to finishing it, but why hurry? Sarajane wouldn't be flying to her grandparents for Thanksgiving as Andy had hoped, so no one would be here to see the mess but his little sister, Laney, who was used to his perpetual projects and didn't mind them in the least.

Sighing softly, Andy picked up the remote control and turned on the television for the noise. He then walked to his bedroom. Recently redecorated with bold-colored drapes and coordinating wallpaper, it now boasted roomy, cedar-lined closets and new furniture, as well as a double dresser, night tables and chest, plus a king-size bed that dominated the entire half of the area. Though a large man, Andy really didn't need a bed that big. He slept alone.

He also ate, cleaned, laundered, read and watched television alone, a state of affairs he'd thought himself finally resigned to, but tonight found intolerable. "What the hell is wrong with me?" Andy muttered aloud, sitting on that expanse of bed bemoaning his uncharacteristic self-pity. The next instant, he answered his own question: for every minute spent with Honey and Travis, he'd earned himself an hour of loneliness.

Was it worth it? Utterly miserable, Andy didn't think so. The remainder of that restless night confirmed it.

So he played it smart on Friday and didn't follow through on each and every urge to drop what he was doing to go inside seeking Honey. He did think about her a lot, though, and wondered if she sat in her workroom at the back of the house as usual, surrounded by books and unable to stop thinking of him....

"Andy?"

He started at the sound of Honey's voice so close and turned to face the sliding patio door where she now stood.

"Do you have a minute you can spare me?"

I have a lifetime, he thought, shocking words that came from nowhere and echoed so loudly in his head he feared he'd uttered them aloud. But her expression never changed, a sure indication he hadn't...thank God. Expelling a long breath to calm his suddenly racing heart, Andy laid down the board he held, wiped his hands down his jeans and slowly crossed the deck.

"I need a favor from you tonight," Honey said when they stood toe-to-toe.

Andy instantly imagined all sorts of wonderful things he could do for her that night...and she for him. "Name them, er it."

"I'm leaving early to take a look at that house for rent. I was wondering if you'd mind dropping Travis by the trailer instead of here after practice."

"Sure." He forced a smile, as disappointed as he was relieved by the simplicity—the harmlessness—of her request. If occasional contact with Honey resulted in hours of loneliness, what would a night of unbridled passion cost him?

"I know it's a lot of bother."

"No bother."

"Thanks so much." Smiling warmly, she turned to step back into the kitchen.

"Hey, Honey with a capital *H*."

She peered over her shoulder at him, still smiling. "Hmm?"

"Any lunch plans today?" The words fell off his tongue, as unbridled as that passion he'd been hoping for.

"Yes, actually. I'm eating with Nicole. She wants to show me her wedding dress."

"So they're really going through with it, huh?" Andy murmured, shaking his head.

Honey bubbled with disbelieving laughter. "Of course they're going through with it. You thought they wouldn't?"

"Nah. I knew they would. They have that look about them. You must know the one I mean...."

"Hopelessly happy?"

"Not exactly."

"Disgustingly dazed?"

"You're getting there."

"Critically crazy?"

"That's it!"

They laughed together, then, the two of them, and just for an instant Andy felt a little crazy himself. Crazy for Honey of the green eyes and magic smile. Crazy, crazy, crazy.

A bit startled by the extent of his lunacy, Andy kept to himself the rest of the day and was actually glad when time for football practice rolled around. As always, he made use of the physical exertion of coaching twenty-three boisterous boys to burn off his frustrations, and by the time he called practice to a halt, he felt downright sane and strong enough to face Honey again.

It was one exhausted, but still enthusiastic Travis who scrambled into his truck that evening along with another boy, Matt Holbrook, whose mother had begged a ride from Andy, as well. Andy listened while the two boys discussed baseball cards, video games and their favorite Saturday cartoons. They next talked about November Nights and their big plans to win a prize at this or that booth at the school festival.

When Andy reached Matt's house, the youngster parted with a "See ya tomorrow night," which could well mean the beginning of a fast friendship. Andy smiled, recalling that his friendships with Jack and Ethan began about this age. He wished the same for Travis.

As she had yesterday afternoon at the library, Honey greeted them at the door, but this time she wasn't smiling. Andy guessed the reason at once. "The house..."

"Was a dump." Her eyes actually glistened with her disappointment, and his heart went out to her.

"Tough luck."

Honey nodded agreement and stepped back to let her son slip through the door into the living room. Andy saw him head over to a bright yellow beanbag chair and plop down in front of the television. Expecting another quick dismissal from Honey, Andy made no move to follow.

"You're not coming in?"

"Well, I really need to go..." *You sure as hell do.* "But if you'd like me to hang around for a while, I guess I could."

"Oh, would you? I'm kind of in a funk." She laughed apologetically. "It might help to ventilate to another adult for a change."

Andy didn't give Honey time to reconsider, but stepped quickly into the tiny trailer.

"You *are* a little cramped in here, aren't you?" he murmured, eyeing the wall-to-wall furniture and a ceiling-high stack of boxes, most likely filled with personal belongings she didn't have room to unpack, much less put away.

"I bump into myself every time I turn around, and I need my furniture," she replied, moving aside a stack of magazines so Andy could sit on a love seat. She looked for a place to set them, found none, and huffed her exasperation before dumping the load onto the floor. She then joined Andy.

He couldn't help but laugh. "My offer to build you a house still stands."

"Thanks...but I'm really not ready for that kind of financial commitment." She sounded so regretful that Andy's heart went right out to her. Apparently he wasn't the only one so moved.

"I know what," Travis suddenly exclaimed, eyes alight with a wonderful idea as he focused on his mom. "We can move in with Coach Fulbright. He's got a great big house—" he shifted his gaze to Andy "—don't you, Coach?"

"Great big," Andy agreed, relishing the sight of Honey, cheeks glowing pink with embarrassment.

"And he wouldn't mind...would you, Coach?" Travis continued.

"Not a bit."

Travis leaped off the beanbag chair. "I'll go pack my baseball cards."

"Whoa there, mister," his mom exclaimed, collaring him. "You'll sit right back down in that chair, is what you'll do. We're not moving in with Coach Fulbright now or ever."

"Why not?" Travis whined.

"Because...because..." Suddenly she leaned over and elbowed Andy in the ribs. "I'm just not up to this tonight. Would you please tell him why?"

Andy, who thought Travis's idea a fine one, absently rubbed his smarting rib while he fumbled through his brain for a reason. "Because we're not a family."

Travis considered that for a moment. "What's a family?"

"Ideally, a mom, a dad and their children," Andy replied without thought.

"What's 'dilly'?" Travis next asked, a question that probably explained his rather grown-up vocabulary.

"*Ideally* means *the best,*" Honey replied. "But I'm not sure that's the word Coach Fulbright should've used. I think *traditional* is probably a better choice. Do you know what *traditional* means?"

Travis who obviously didn't know *or* care, shook his head rather impatiently. "So if Coach was my dad we could live in his house?"

"Ye-e-s. But remember, honey, you already have a dad back in Boston."

"You mean Charlie?" Travis asked.

Surprised to hear Travis call his father by his first name, Andy glanced at Honey to gauge her reaction.

"Of course I mean Charlie," she said, caught off guard more by the question than the name, in Andy's judgment.

"He doesn't count."

"Why not?" Honey was puzzled by his assertion.

Her son huffed his exasperation with her stupidity. "We divorced him and moved away."

"Travis, honey, just because Charlie's not my husband anymore doesn't mean he's not your dad...even if we did move from Boston."

"But he doesn't come to see me."

Visibly disconcerted, Travis's mother glanced quickly at Andy before slipping off the couch to kneel next to the beanbag. She took her son's hand in hers. "He's awfully busy." She paused as though struggling to find a truth that wouldn't hurt. "And our living here in Alabama does make it hard for him to visit." Travis considered that, but said nothing. "I'm sure he'll come to see you one of these days, though." Honey's voice trembled, and her distress produced a lump of sympathy in Andy's throat. All at once, he found himself wanting to make everything better for her and Travis.

"I have an idea," he blurted out, words that earned him the immediate attention of Travis and a hopeful glance from Honey. "Since your dad and my daughter are so far away, you and I will just have to help each other out some."

Travis's eyes rounded in surprise. "You've got a little kid, too?"

"I sure do," Andy told him. "Her name is Sarajane. She lives in France with her mother. We're divorced . . . just like your mom and Charlie are."

"So I can be your boy sometimes, and you can be my dad sometimes?"

"I don't see why not."

Travis smiled from ear to ear, an expression that evolved into a frown only seconds later.

"What's wrong now?" Honey asked.

"I'm wond'rin' who can be your husband," Travis answered in his disconcertingly grown-up way. He proceeded to give the matter considerable thought.

Honey laughed and waved both hands. "Oh, don't worry about me—" she began, only to halt when Travis suddenly smiled again. "Don't tell me you've thought of someone already?"

"Uh-huh," her son replied as he pointed to Andy. "You can be his wife sometimes, and he can be your husband sometimes."

"Great idea!" Andy exclaimed, slapping his knee. He stared at Honey until she raised her gaze to his. Grinning at her, he stood. "And now that we've settled that, I think I'd better get on home. I'll see you tomorrow at the game, sometimes son, and you, too, sometimes wife."

Giggling at Andy's foolishness, Travis leaped up from his seat and ran over to hug him. "Come see me whenever you want."

Swallowing hard, Andy patted his dark hair thankfully, then eased free and walked to the door, Honey on his heels.

"That was very kind of you," she whispered, eyes shining, as he stepped outside into the dusk.

"Kindness was not my motive," he replied, pausing on the top step, turning back to stand nose-to-nose with her.

"I need Travis as much as he needs me. As for his mommy..."

"Yes?" Honey prompted when he hesitated.

"I need her, too. The question is, does she need me?"

"Sometimes," Honey replied with a wistful smile.

"Sometimes," Andy echoed softly. "That word again. I have a pretty good idea about the duties of a sometimes dad, but I'm having a little trouble figuring out what a sometimes husband does."

"Oh, that's easy," she told him. "Take out the trash, fix the leaky faucet, mow the lawn, wash the—"

"Wife's back?"

"Actually, I was going to say car, but I guess some husbands do scrub their wives' backs for them."

"When?"

"When what?"

"When do you want me to scrub yours?"

"Never. I have a back scrubber that works very well."

"What's his name?" Andy asked.

Honey, who'd been thinking of a plain plastic brush with a long handle and soft bristles, blinked in surpise at the question, then rose to the challenge of his teasing. "I can only tell you this. My back scrubber is always handy, always ready, and does a very thorough job."

Andy whistled softly through his teeth. "That's a tough act to follow."

Honey laughed. "Yes."

"But I'd still like to try."

"You would?" Andy saw her convulsive swallow.

"Oh, yeah. I would."

She exhaled a shaky breath, then turned serious eyes on him. "This kind of idiocy isn't helping our situation."

"No," Andy agreed.

"If we were smart, we'd make a pact with each other to clean up our act, and we'd shake hands to make that pact binding."

"I'd rather seal it with a kiss."

"Andy!"

"Okay, okay. I admit there's a problem, but I refuse to make another pact."

"Another... Oh, yeah. That one with your friends."

"That one with my friends," Andy agreed with a nod. "The one that made everyone's life miserable."

"So what do you suggest?"

"I suggest we quit stewing so much about this. I'm a guy—you're a gal. We're both free. If we're attracted to one another, then what the hell? Give me one good reason why we shouldn't be."

Honey said nothing for a moment, clearly lost in thought.

"Well?" Andy prompted.

"I can think of lots of reasons," she admitted, "but none of them are good."

"Then could we please quit jawing about this and just see what happens?"

She considered his suggestion, then shrugged. "If you'd like."

"And what about you? What would you like?"

"I'd like to spend time with you and not worry about whether or not I'm doing the right thing."

"Then do it."

"But what about my bad marriage? What about yours? What about Travis?" Honey peeked over her shoulder at her son, mesmerized by something on the television.

"Our bad marriages are irrelevant. We're not looking for lifetime commitment here, just a little fun. As for

Travis... you don't have to worry about him. I'd never do anything to hurt your son, Honey. Never."

"I know that."

"So why don't we both just relax? Face each moment as it happens and do what has to be done."

"I suppose we could." She sounded rather doubtful.

"You don't seem very excited about this."

Honey smiled ruefully at him. "If I don't, it's nothing personal. I really do like you, Andy... a lot... and I want to get to know you better."

"Ditto," he told her, adding, "I guess this particular moment of our relationship is our Declaration of Independence from old fears, huh?"

Honey smiled at the idea. "I guess it is."

"We should probably celebrate with fireworks, don't you think?"

"Definitely, but I don't have any around. Do you?"

"No. How about we do the next best thing?"

"Which is...?"

"Kiss me," Andy whispered, stepping close and touching his lips to hers before she could nix his action. At first he took care to keep Honey square between him and Travis so the child couldn't see. His rising passion quickly got the better of him, though, and with a soft growl of frustration, he wrapped his arms around Honey, lifted her right off her feet, and stepped to the side, out of view of the living room, if not the world.

Safe from Travis's innocent eyes, he then deepened the kiss by teasing Honey's mouth open wide with his tongue so he could probe and savor the sweet interior. She cooperated in every way and then did some tasting of her own, demonstrating that her hunger equaled his.

"Aren't they beautiful?" Andy whispered between nibbles to her cheek, chin and neck.

"What do you mean?" Honey breathed and then gasped when his mouth found her earlobe.

"The fireworks, babe. Aren't they something?"

Honey caught his face in her hands, framing it, and raising his gaze to hers. Their eyes locked. "They're something special, Andy. Something very, very special."

Andy stared at her for a moment, basking in the warmth of her gaze and her smile. His heart did a back flip that left him breathless and a little disoriented. "Yeah. Well, I guess I've done enough husbandly chores for tonight. Will I see you tomorrow at the game?"

"Of course."

He walked backward a few steps, his gaze locked with hers, then turned and crossed the remaining distance to his truck. God, how good it felt to be around a woman again. And if the few kisses they'd shared could make him so mellow, imagine what more time with Honey could do. Why, he'd soon be his old self again—optimistic, happy-go-lucky. There'd be no more scurrying to fill his every waking moment with activity such as his nighttime workouts at the gym, his house remodeling, his coaching.

Andy stopped short and whirled around to find that Honey still stood at her door, watching him. "Would you and Travis like to ride with me to the game tomorrow?"

"Why, we'd love to," she replied.

"Three o'clock?"

"We'll be ready."

And so will I, he thought, mentally rubbing his palms together in anticipation of being with her again. With a wave, he got into his truck and drove away. Honey stood in the doorway, staring at her empty drive for several long moments after he left, still a little dazed from the kiss, not to mention the astounding conversation that preceded it.

With a sigh of who-knew-what, she turned to find Travis standing behind her, his eyes solemn, his face thoughtful.

Had he seen anything? she wondered, even as she asked, "Hungry?"

He nodded.

"What sounds good to you?" She bustled over to the kitchen, a matter of two short steps, and began to peruse the cabinets for something to feed Travis. And still he said nothing. "How about tuna sandwiches?"

He shrugged unenthusiastically.

"Chicken noodle soup?"

Another shrug.

"Bacon and eggs?"

Yet another, and his expression never changed.

What's going on in that head? Honey wondered with growing unease. "You're awfully quiet."

"I'm thinkin'."

"About what?" Honey asked, making a dinner decision for him by opening the can of soup.

"Charlie." Travis had called his father Charlie ever since the tender age of two. Honey wasn't sure why, but secretly believed it was because the three of them lived with Charlie's parents at the time and his mother had called out for him constantly.

Honey poured the soup into a pan and set it on the stove to heat. After taking a stirring spoon out of the drawer, she walked over to squat down so she could be eye level with her son. "So you're thinking about your father."

"Uh-huh. I don't want him to come and see us."

"Why not?"

"'Cause you might get married to him again."

Honey shook her head. "I think you're forgetting that Charlie's married to someone else. Remember Loretta?"

Travis thought hard for a minute, then slowly nodded. "The lady with the white cat?"

"Yes. She's Charlie's wife now, and even if she weren't, I wouldn't marry him again. We just aren't compatible."

"What's "patible'?"

Honey, who usually encouraged her son's constant search for definitions, sighed wearily. "*Compatible* is when people get along together."

"Like you and Coach Fulbright?"

"Oh, I don't know that we're such a good example...."

"But you kissed him."

Honey's heart skipped a beat. "Saw that, did you?"

Travis nodded.

"Hmm. Well, would you do me a big favor and not tell anyone?"

"You mean you, me and Coach will have a secret?"

"A big secret. Are you old enough to keep it?"

Travis nodded solemnly.

"Thanks, and just so you understand about me and Coach, we get along well enough to kiss sometimes, but not near well enough to get married. Now does that answer your question?"

"I guess so," Travis said, his little shoulders slumping.

"What's wrong now?" Honey asked, though she had a good idea.

"I want Coach to be my dad."

"He will be...*sometimes*. Remember your agreement?"

"But I want him all the time."

"That would be nice, wouldn't it?" Honey murmured.

Travis nodded.

"It can't be that way, though, so I guess we'll just have to make the most of the times he's ours. Okay?"

"Okay."

Honey reached out and pulled her son close, absently patting his back much as she'd done when he was an infant. To her surprise, he didn't try to escape as he'd been doing more and more these days.

"Smells like your soup's done," she said when he'd finally had enough of being cuddled and pulled away long minutes later. She stood and walked to the stove. "Go wash up." Travis did and then returned to climb onto one of the two chairs at the kitchen table. Honey handed him a bowl of steaming soup. "Eat up so you'll be strong for your game tomorrow."

Travis began to eat obediently, but with little enthusiasm. "Are you gonna be there to watch me play?"

"Why, I wouldn't miss it for the world."

"I have to be there early. Maybe I should ride with Coach so you can come later."

"We're both riding with Coach, Travis," Honey said as she joined him at the table, her own bowl and spoon in hand. "He's picking us up."

Travis's eyes widened as did the smile that suddenly appeared on his face. *"He is?"*

"Yes."

"All right!"

Honey nearly choked on her soup at the sound of Travis's joyful exclamation.

All right? Was "all right" really a term that could be aptly applied to a sometimes relationship with Andy

Fulbright when her precious son, not to mention she, could be hurt so easily?

Not by a long shot, Honey realized with sudden dismay.

Abruptly she pushed her soup away. There was another phrase—a more appropriate phrase—to describe a liaison with Andy: all *wrong!* And no matter how badly she or Travis needed a man such as Andy in their lives, she'd be nothing but a fool if she pretended otherwise.

Chapter Five

Travis's football game proved to be rather interesting, even though Honey didn't know the rules. A people watcher from day one, she occupied herself studying the pint-size players and equally pint-size cheerleaders, the other parents and, yes, Coach Andy Fulbright.

So what if she had no business staring at him—especially after last night's realization that letting him into her life probably wasn't the smartest thing she'd ever done. No woman could keep her eyes off a specimen such as Andy.

And for that reason, Honey, seated on the bleachers among strangers, only pretended to watch the game when her son wasn't on the field. In reality, she focused her gaze on the strategically situated, utterly masculine curves and bulges of Andy's faded formfitting jeans.

My oh my, but he made her remember how nice it was to have a man of one's own around. True, she and her ex-man, Charlie, hadn't gotten along all that well. But even the worst marriages had once had their good moments—those asexual instances of total communication and companionship—and the better she got to know Andy, the more she remembered and longed for their return. She didn't long for Charlie, of course. Didn't even long for Andy in particular. Any male-type person would do.

"Yeah, right," Honey muttered under her breath, grimacing. Who was she trying to kid? It was Andy, and Andy alone, she wanted to hang out with. Andy of the dark blue eyes and temptingly touchable tush.

Asexual? Ha!

With a sigh, Honey jerked her attention back to the game and her son, now on the field. He must be doing okay, she decided. He certainly looked like one of the bunch, and because he did, she didn't have any problems congratulating him on a game well played when it ended just after four o'clock.

Since they had to be at the grade school by five o'clock, Honey had to refuse her son's request to stay for the next, and last, game of the day so he could watch some of his school friends play. They had no more practices or games until the week after next because of the upcoming holiday.

"You don't mind if we don't stay, do you?" she asked Andy as an afterthought, wishing she'd brought her own vehicle.

"Not at all," he said and then led the way to his truck.

They arrived at the trailer mere minutes later, and to Honey's surprise, Andy got out of his truck instead of just dropping her and her son off. Surely he didn't plan to come in.... But apparently he did and followed them to the door.

"How about a glass of lemonade?" Honey offered, not wanting to be rude to the coach who'd been such a help with Travis all week.

"Thanks."

"I'll have to ask you to serve yourself," she said in an inspired attempt to let him know she was in a hurry. "Travis needs to take a quick bath and get into some clean clothes before we leave."

"That's fine," Andy replied, moving to help himself to a glass and some lemonade instead of taking her hint and leaving as she'd hoped.

With a shake of her head that Andy didn't see, Honey grasped her son's shoulders and nudged him to the bathroom where clean clothes already lay waiting. She filled the tub while she helped him out of his football gear, then ordered him into the water with a firm "Hurry."

She did little more for herself than change into nicer pants and a shirt and twist her hair up, then walked back to the kitchen to find Andy seated at the dinette, looking for all the world as though he expected supper shortly.

Honey felt a stab of guilt. "There are some chocolate chip cookies." She pointed to a plate with a dozen or so on it. "I had a few too brown to take to the cake walk tonight."

"Really?" Apparently undaunted by the almost burned rims of the cookies, Andy ate several while Honey began to load up her car with the wreaths she had made all week. Andy, his mouth full of cookie,jumped to her aid, saying briskly, "I'll get those."

And he did, making several trips to her car. Honey used the time saved to make sure her son had washed properly and then to help him into his clothes. He talked about November Nights the whole time, telling her what he and his friend, Matt, planned to do.

"Is Matt's mother going to be with you two, then?" Honey asked hopefully. That would certainly alleviate her worries about Travis's wandering through November Nights unchaperoned.

"Nah—"

"No, ma'am," Honey interjected.

"No, ma'am," Travis dutifully echoed. "His mom is working at the cake walk all night."

So much for that idea. "So you two are going to go around with Matt's dad, then."

"Matt doesn't have a dad."

Great. "I'm not too sure about this, son," Honey had to say.

"'Bout what?" Travis asked, raising his arms so she could slip on his blue knit shirt.

"About you and Matt walking around November Nights alone."

"But we won't be alone. We'll be together."

"I know that, Travis," she replied, lifting him to stand on the lowered toilet seat so she could comb his damp hair. "But I'm still worried, and I'm thinking you need to stay with me tonight... at least until I rope someone into watching the handicraft room for a few minutes. We'll explore then."

"But, Mom," Travis argued, "me and Matt already planned what we're going to do."

"I know, and I'm really sorry, son."

"It's not fair!" her son wailed. "I never get to do anything."

"You do, too," Honey retorted, fast losing patience and not necessarily because her son's request was unreasonable. It wasn't really, and her knowing that only made things worse since she was helpless to give him what he wanted.

"It's not fair! It's not fair!" Travis began to cry now, great sobs that twisted Honey's heart and brought Andy on the run.

"What's wrong?" he demanded from the bathroom door.

"Mom won't let me go to November Nights!"

"You're not taking him with you?" Andy asked before Honey could correct her son.

With a sniff of exasperation, Honey tossed her comb onto the counter and set her son down on the floor. "Of course I'm taking him with me. I'm just not going to let him wander all over the place with Matt, that's all." She brushed past him and headed to the kitchen.

"But Matt's a good kid," Andy said, following her with Travis on his heels.

"So is Travis," Honey said, turning to confront him. "But that doesn't mean I can let them wander around for three hours without adult supervision. I have to work tonight, you know."

That got Andy's attention. He looked down at Travis. "Matt's Mom's not going to be there?"

"She's working, too," Honey replied for her son. She snatched up her purse and their jackets. "Now I hate to be rude, but we really have to go."

"I don't want to go!" Travis retorted, dragging his feet when she tried to hustle him to the door.

"Well, that's tough, mister," Honey said, grabbing him by the arm. "Because you are, and you're going to behave, too."

"Hold on!" Andy suddenly exclaimed. "Wait a minute! I have the answer!"

Both Honey and her son looked back at Andy in astonishment.

He grinned. "*I'll* escort the boys around November Nights."

"You will?" Travis exclaimed and grinned from ear to ear.

"Sure I will." Andy tousled Travis's freshly combed hair, and they both laughed.

"I can't ask you to do that," Honey said, instinctively reaching to smooth her son's raven locks.

"You *aren't* asking me. I'm volunteering. Now do you want to be late?" He put a hand to the small of her back and urged her toward the door.

"N-No."

"Then let's go."

And so they did go—in Honey's car. Andy and Travis found Matt the moment they stepped into the lobby of the elementary school. Several other boys waited, too, and all were delighted to learn that Coach intended to hang around with them. By the time Honey headed down the hall to the handicraft room, the "men" had all vanished in the other direction.

That was the last time Honey had a spare moment since the handicraft room attracted scores of customers. A classroom by day, the area had been furnished with tables and shelves on which were heaped every kind of handicraft imaginable from hand-painted Christmas cards to homemade jams and jellies.

Honey, thankful for the chance to meet some of the townspeople who would visit the library once it had opened, greeted each person warmly. Business boomed, and involved as she was in selling all the wonderful items donated by parents and teachers, she didn't have time to eat, worry about her son, or even make a trip to the bathroom until...

"Hi there."

Honey started at the sound of that greeting, spoken directly into her ear by a very familiar male voice. "Hi, yourself," she said, glancing over her shoulder at him. "I figured Travis and his friends would have you roped and tied to a tree in the school yard by now."

"*Moi?* You forget to whom you speak, Madam Librarian," Andy replied with a grin. "I'm the guy who can make them run laps and do push-ups at football practice if they don't behave."

Honey had to laugh. "I did forget."

"Yes, and there's something else you forgot, too," he said, holding out a hot dog and a cola.

"Actually, I just haven't had time," she told him.

"Well, take time now. One of the parents has relieved me, so I'll relieve you."

"Are you kidding?" she asked with a laugh.

"I am not," he told her. He glanced around the room. "How hard can this be?"

"Not hard at all." Honey slid off her stool. "And I'm sure you'll do a wonderful job." She moved toward the door, her boots clicking against the tile floor.

"Wait!" Andy called out. He held up the hot dog and soft drink. "Don't you want your dinner?"

"After I make a pit stop," Honey said and then, accompanied by the sound of his laughter, exited and headed to the nearest little girls' room. Moments later, she returned to the handicraft room and scooped up the drink and hot dog Andy had left on the desk. Since he now stood at the far side of the room in conversation with a very attractive young woman, Honey sat on her stool once more and nibbled on the food.

Try as she might to keep her eyes off the handsome carpenter, they strayed to him more than once, taking admiring note of the way his forest green shirt stretched tautly over his shoulders and narrowed at his waist. He was a sight for sure.

As for the woman, Honey found herself appraising her with curiosity tinted by what could only be jealousy. Surprised by the emotion, she took a mental step back and analyzed it.

Or tried to. There was really no excuse for resenting the attention Andy paid to another female. It wasn't as though the two of them really had anything going between them. And Andy didn't look particularly entertained by the woman, anyway. In fact, he'd been edging his way back to her stool for several minutes now. Unfortunately, the woman kept hampering his efforts by blocking his path with her very shapely body, oh-so-enticingly encased in black leotard, matching tights and a leopard-skin-print jacket.

Suddenly, to Honey's surprise, Andy looked up as if he'd just noticed her—even though they'd made eye contact several times since her return. He walked quickly over to where she sat. The woman followed more slowly.

"Hey, Honey," he said in such a way that Honey actually wondered if the *H* was a capital. "Didn't see you come back. Did you get enough to eat?"

"Plenty, thanks." She smiled toward Andy's companion. "Hi. I'm Honorine Truman."

"Marcie Mabry," the woman, a brunette with gorgeous, assessing blue eyes, murmured.

"Do you have a child at Winterhaven Elementary?" Honey asked.

"Oh, no," Marcie replied with an airy laugh. "No children." That explained her flat tummy. "I just came for the...diversion. You know how little there is to do in a town this size." She smiled, but not with those azure eyes, and turned to Andy. "At the risk of soundng crude,

I must ask. Is *Honorine* the reason you won't leave with me? I mean . . . if you two are a pair, you should just say so."

"Oh, we're not a pair," Honey denied, to help Andy out. If he'd refused to leave with such a striking woman, it had to be because of his promise to look after Travis. She intended to let him off the hook now.

"Too late, Honey," Andy abruptly interjected. "Marcie has obviously figured us out."

With a self-satisfied smirk, Marcie turned her gaze on Honey, whose jaw had dropped at Andy's astonishing answer. "Don't look so surprised, dear. I have a sixth sense where relationships are concerned. You just can't fool me. Luckily, no one else around here has a clue, so your secret is safe."

"We surely appreciate that," Andy smoothly responded. "We'd really like to keep this to ourselves for a while yet."

"You can count on me," Marcie told him, then added, "and if you two, um, split the sheet, can *I* count on *you?*"

"To . . ."

"To give me a call."

"Oh." Now Andy looked as disconcerted as Honey felt. "Sure. I'll give you a call."

"Good." She smiled again and walked to the door. "See you around," she said before vanishing out into the hall.

Honey sat in stunned silence for a moment, staring at Andy. Finally she found the right words. "Are you crazy?"

"Actually, *desperate* is probably a better description," he replied with a shrug. "That woman's been after me for months." He shivered as though in horror. "But this should do the trick."

"That's not all *this* might do," Honey exclaimed, hopping off her stool and standing toe-to-toe with him. Oblivious to everyone but the two of them, she poked her forefinger in his chest, just about heart-high. "What if she doesn't keep her mouth shut, Andy Fulbright? What if she tells any and everyone what you've told her?"

Andy glanced over her head and around the room, an action that should have alerted Honey to the possibility of an audience, but didn't. "We'll set them straight."

"Set them—" Honey rolled her eyes at his naiveté. Didn't he know how difficult it was to correct an inaccurate rumor? "Forget it," she exclaimed, her voice rising in agitation. "No matter what either of us says or does, we'll be sharing a bed tonight and engaged by next week."

She referred to the stories she soon expected to hear circulating, of course, and was surprised when Andy's eyes began to twinkle. Obviously he didn't realize the gravity of their situation. She simply couldn't afford any scandal that might compromise the success of the library.

"This isn't a bit amusing."

"Oh, I don't know..." he murmured, glancing over her head again. This time the action registered. Honey tensed and risked a look over her shoulder to find the room filled to capacity with very interested customers.

Mortified, she snapped her head back to meet Andy's gaze. "Damn."

He laughed then and kissed her. Right on the mouth. In front of God and who knew who. But what did it matter? A kiss so chaste was mere icing on the cake of humiliation she had baked for herself this night.

Not surprisingly, the evening slid downhill from that point on. Honey did her best to act normally after Andy left her a short time later, but failed miserably since every time she made a sale she found herself wondering if her customer thought she was Andy Fulbright's mistress.

Closing time finally arrived. With great relief, Honey counted the money and turned it over to the November Nights coordinator. With the help of Travis and Andy, she then boxed up the thankfully few items that hadn't sold and locked them in a storage closet as previously instructed.

Not a bit too soon, the three of them stepped out into the chilly night. A short drive later found them at the trailer once more. Travis, utterly exhausted, didn't even argue when Honey made short work of undressing him so he could crawl into bed. Moments after she tucked him in, she heard his steady breathing, a sure sign that he was asleep.

Bone-tired, too, it was all Honey could do to drag herself to the living room, where Andy sat on the love seat watching the late news. He looked up when she walked over, then patted the cushion next to his. Honey accepted the invitation and settled down beside him.

They sat in silence for a moment, both watching the television and, in Honey's case, resting. Just as she began to relax a little, Andy reached out and laid an arm across her shoulders, a move that sent her pulse into hyperdrive.

Instantly wired again, she cleared her throat and tried to make normal conversation. "Travis had a wonderful time. Thanks for taking care of him."

"My pleasure," Andy murmured, turning his head to place a kiss in her hair before loosening the pins that held it securely on the top of her head.

Honey gulped and remembered her unintentional prediction about what would happen between them tonight. At once, sharing a bed seemed like a wonderful idea. He sat so close and smelled so good....

"You're a good sometimes father—a rarity in my opinion," she commented. "Most men can't be bothered with Saturday afternoon football games and Saturday night school festivals."

"Most, you say?" Andy shook his head and began to play with her hair. "Not most. *Some,* maybe, but not most."

"I suppose you're right," Honey softly agreed, relaxing in stages until her bones felt as limp as rope. "I do have a tendency to judge men based on my experience with Charlie."

"Tell me about Charlie," Andy said. "How did you two meet?"

"I worked as a librarian at the museum his mother patronized. He came to a board meeting with his mother. We met, fell in love, had an affair, started a baby and then married, all within a year."

"So what happened?" He'd stopped fingering her hair and now was twisting it around his index finger.

"We moved into his parents' mansion, had the baby and divorced... all within the next year."

"I'm terribly sorry," Andy said, giving her a little hug, most likely of sympathy. Honey's heart thumped hard against her chest.

"Me, too. I had such big plans." She laughed softly and without real humor. "Poor Charlie. I guess he had big plans, too. Unfortunately, they weren't the same as mine."

"So what are your plans now?" Andy moved his arm from across her shoulders and leaned forward slightly to rest his elbows on his knees. "Surely you haven't eliminated a happily-forever-after from them."

"No, but I will take different steps to attain it."

"Different steps?"

"Perhaps I should reword that." Honey thought for a moment. "Let's just say I won't marry for love... but we've established that already, haven't we?" She stood and walked to the kitchen to get herself something to drink. "Would you like a beer? I have some stashed away."

"Yes, thanks," he said. Honey retrieved two cans from a bin in the refrigerator and walked back to the love seat to hand him one.

"What about you, Andy Fulbright? As I'm sure Marcie will agree, you're a prize catch with your steady job, long-distance ex and love of children. Are you going to make some woman deliriously happy one of these days?"

"If I can find one who'll marry for the same reasons as me."

"And what are those, if I might ask?" She settled on the opposite end of the love seat, slipped off her boots and turned, bending her knees so she could rest her stockinged feet on the cushion between them. To her surprise, Andy reached out and lifted her feet so that they rested on his lap.

"Number one," he replied. "I want a woman who will cherish her role as wife and mother."

"She can't work outside the home?"

"I never said that. I learned the hard way that women have as much right to a career as men do."

"You didn't want Jaclyn to work?"

"No, and my selfishness resulted in a rebellion that ruined our marriage."

"Hmm," Honey murmured, impressed by his honesty. "Well, my number one is similar. I want a man who will take his role as husband, father and provider very seriously."

Andy considered that a moment. "Makes sense. Now to number two. I want a woman who wants children."

"Me, too," Honey absently agreed. "Er, a man, that is."

Andy nodded. "And last but never least, there's number three, which is an offshoot of number two and should probably be called two and a half. I want a woman who loves sex—anytime, anywhere, anyhow."

Honorine, who'd just taken a drink, nearly choked to death before she got the mouthful of foaming brew swallowed. She then coughed for several minutes while Andy pounded her on the back.

"May I take it that your number three is different from mine?"

"You may," she told him with a sniff. "I want a man who's kind."

"I see. Do you have a number four?"

"Mmm-hmm. I want a man who's honest."

"And number five?"

Honey set her half-empty can on the floor. "I want a man who doesn't smoke."

"Isn't good sex even on your list?" Andy suddenly demanded, frowning.

"Sure it is . . . somewhere . . . and what difference does it make, anyway?"

"No difference. No difference at all. It just seems odd that a woman who kisses the way you do doesn't like sex."

Honey sat bolt upright. "I never said I didn't like sex. In fact, if you'll recall, I've admitted that I'm very attracted to you."

"So sexual compatibility is pretty important in a husband?"

"Yes, of course, but difficult to discern unless one experiments."

"So what's wrong with experimentation?" Andy asked, absently plucking at the upturned cuff of her pants. "Scientists do it all the time."

"They do, indeed, but remember, I've experimented before and know the results can't always be trusted. That's why sex is so low on my list, Andy, not because I don't like it."

"Oh." He sat in silence for a moment, then gave her a solemn nod. "Well, anytime you change your mind, just give me a call. I minored in science in college. I'm great in the lab."

I'll bet you are, Honey thought, her head filled with a vision of the two of them, experimenting together. The fantasy set her heart to racing, and to hide her reaction, she feigned a yawn.

"Tired?" Andy asked.

"Exhausted."

"Then I'll go." He set her feet off his lap and stood, reaching down to help her up. Together they walked to the door.

"Thanks a million for coming tonight," she said. "You made Travis very happy."

"He returned the favor a hundredfold," Andy answered. He stepped out the door, but walked no farther than the edge of the porch before stopping, turning and facing her. "Sure you're not into experimentation? We'll do it the right way...no risk involved."

"There's always risk," Honey reminded him. "No matter how careful you are."

"Yeah," he said, "I guess there is." He stepped onto the grass, then paused again. "See you on Monday?"

"Bright and early."

He made it all the way to his truck this time before he halted. "Can I talk you into one little kiss? I mean... we've done that before with no ill effects...well, not many, anyway."

Laughing softly, Honey joined him by the truck. "One little kiss should be harmless enough."

In a heartbeat, Andy pulled her into his arms and covered her mouth with his in a hungry, hungry kiss that could be called many things, but never harmless. His tongue swept over her teeth, probing for entry. Honey's gasp allowed it, and she gloried in this one intimacy that was all she dared.

The man was dangerous. Very dangerous. And it wouldn't take many kisses for him to realize that she hadn't been totally honest when sharing her feelings about sex. There were times when it ranked high on her list of musts. Times when she had no qualms about experimenting.

Now was one of them.

"I...have...to...go...in," she somehow managed to tell him, her breathless words muffled by his lips on hers.

He pulled back slightly, breaking the contact. "Right this minute?"

"Now." She stepped away, took several deep breaths and darted to the safety of the porch. "Good night, Andy. Sleep tight."

Instead of replying, he laughed as though there was no possible way. A few moments later, his truck's taillights vanished into the dark.

For all their tense parting on Saturday night, the next two weeks passed with amazing normalcy and actually took on a pleasant pattern that Andy cherished.

He saw Honey several times a day, every day, and then worked with Travis on the practice field in the afternoons. Both Saturdays, they rode together to the games, sharing a meal afterward whether it was a morning or an afternoon game.

Their togetherness naturally produced a few raised eyebrows, and with growing frequency friends asked Andy to verify a rumor that he and Honorine were an item—a sure indication that Marcie or someone else had talked. Andy usually kept his cool and assured them that there wasn't any truth to the rumor.

He wasn't alone in these inquisitions. Honey admitted that she'd had to address the rumor, too, but reassured Andy that she'd only said that he was good for Travis and vice versa. Surprisingly the gossip didn't bother either of them much, a fact for which Andy was grateful. He didn't want anything to jeopardize their friendship.

Friendship? Well . . . not exactly. Andy and Honey always parted with a more-than-friendly kiss—at least when Travis was out of sight. Those kisses inevitably left him aching for more, and if he could've talked her into it, Andy probably wouldn't have minded expanding the friendship to include sharing a bed.

That was quite an achievement for a man, who, less than a year ago, had sworn off women. But Honey was just so special—a selfless mother who made every effort, every sacrifice to provide her son with a stable home life. Sometimes when thinking about her, Andy unwittingly thought of Jaclyn.

For all her faults, Jaclyn took the role of mother quite seriously, too, and had probably not been lying when she claimed she challenged Andy's original custody rights only because she didn't want Sarajane shuffled from continent to continent so often. And while he still hadn't forgiven her, he admitted to a certain softening of attitude that he credited to Honey's influence.

On Sunday, fifteen days after November Nights, the ringing of the telephone woke Andy from an inadvertent nap on his recliner. Muttering an oath—he'd slept through the whole last half of the football game on cable—Andy snatched up the receiver and growled a hello.

A moment's startled silence followed the greeting. "Uh, Andy?"

"Honey...what's up?" They'd never visited on a Sunday for some reason. It was almost as though by unspoken agreement they avoided each other on that one day. Andy didn't know her reasons, but freely admitted to himself that he needed the time off as a sort of cool-down, get-ready-for-another-week-of-temptation sort of day.

"I think I've found a house."

"The Richardson place?" Abe Richardson, high school principal, had suddenly retired last week due to poor health. He and his wife were moving to Phoenix for the dryer climate, and had agreed to show Honey their house.

"No. That one was lovely, but much too expensive. This house is on Maple Street. It's small, brick, with a fenced-in backyard. Do you know it?"

"The only one I can think of is Coy Watson's rental house."

"That's it!"

Andy flicked off the television. "I thought someone already lived in that house."

"They flew the coop owing Coy three months' rent. He called me as soon as he realized it."

"So you're going to rent, huh?"

"For now."

Andy stood up and grinned into the phone. "Why, that's great. Congratulations."

"Thank you," Honey said, her voice jubilant. Andy could just picture her sitting in her tiny living room, Garfield telephone to her ear. "And now to the reason I called. Would you mind checking out the place structurally? I don't know a thing about wood, pipes and electricity."

"Won't those be your landlord's problem?"

"Yes, but I'd feel better if I knew everything was okay. I don't want to get caught in a bad lease. I mean . . . what if those other renters didn't pay Coy for a reason?"

"You do have a point," Andy said. "But I'm afraid I know as little about plumbing and electricity as you do. I do know about foundations, though, and I'll bet I can talk Jack into inspecting everything else."

"Oh, would you call him?"

"Sure."

"Today?"

Hot damn! Honey on a Sunday. "You want us to do this today?"

"Well, I do have the key right now and . . ."

"Today it is. I'll meet you there at, say, three?"

"Perfect. Thanks a million."

A million whats? Andy wondered, hanging up the phone. Hugs? Kisses? Nights?

Laughing at his foolishness, he picked up the receiver again and dialed Jack's number. Luckily he was free, too, and seconds later agreed to meet the three of them at Coy's place.

They found the interior of the house cluttered and dirty, but structurally sound from flooring to pipes. While Honey and Travis danced a jig of pure joy in the spacious living room, Jack dragged Andy aside.

"I thought the two of you were...you know...involved. I figured you'd be getting married soon, maybe even double with Ethan and Nicole."

Andy's jaw dropped. "Married? I know there are a lot of rumors circulating, but surely you, of all people, don't think I'm going to get married again any time soon. My God, Jack, have you already forgotten Ethan and Nicole's engagement party?" Unable to bear watching the demise of their best friend, they'd left early to watch boxing, of all things, on television.

Jack just laughed. "You talk a good game, but I've known the truth about you for years."

"The truth?"

"You're a marrying man."

Andy snorted at the idea even though he knew very well that Jack was right. "And you're crazy."

"Oh, look, you guys, there's a bluebird in the backyard!" Honey's cry broke up their friendly disagreement and drew them to the bay window in the dining room.

"There's a cardinal, too!" Travis exclaimed. Turning to his mother, he tugged on the hem of her oversize sweatshirt. "Can we move in here tonight?"

"We have to clean the place up first, but I promise we'll be in here by Thanksgiving. We'll ask Granny and Gramps to come eat turkey with us, and maybe Skip will come, too, and bring his truck so we can get our furniture out of storage."

"Skip?" Andy asked.

"My baby brother."

"I didn't know you had a brother," Andy said.

"Well, I do, and you're invited to eat dinner with us to meet him and my parents."

"Actually, I was hoping you and Travis would eat with me. My sister, Laney, is coming up. I'm smoking a turkey."

"Oh." She shrugged. "I guess we'll have to be content with just meeting each other's family since we won't get to eat together, huh?"

"Looks that way," Andy agreed with real regret. He'd envisioned the four of them at his dinner table, giving thanks for the meal and for each other.

"Come outside with me!" Travis grabbed his mom's hand and led her, laughing, out the back door.

The moment the screen door slammed shut behind them, Jack placed a hand on Andy's shoulder, leaned forward and chanted, loud, clear and directly into his ear, the words, "Marrying man. Marrying man."

"Go to hell," Andy snapped, not a bit amused that his friend knew of his self-admitted, much-hated weakness.

Such directions didn't bother Jack. He'd heard them countless times before and merely chortled with obvious enjoyment of Andy's predicament.

And a predicament it was, too, Andy realized later that same night when alone in his house once more. What little enthusiasm he'd had for Thanksgiving seemed to be fading fast. First Sarajane and now Honey and Travis would not be there for the feast he planned. If Laney bailed out—and there was always a chance she would make up with her last fiancé—then he'd be forced to spend the holiday alone.

The mere idea stole his usual good humor and threatened the few moments he shared with Honey on the Monday preceding Thanksgiving. Since Nicole had talked her into taking the week off to move, she stopped by the library only long enough to pick up some papers she needed.

Already missing her by the time he dropped Travis off after practice, Andy actually volunteered to help clean up the house, only to be told that Coy "Skinflint" Watson had actually hired someone to do it. Andy then offered to help her pack, but was informed that her parents were arriving that very night and her brother on Wednesday. Since they'd all be in town until Thursday afternoon, he could only surmise that he'd see next to nothing of her until after she completed the move.

Relegated once more to the fringes of Honey's life, a state of affairs he used to consider adequate, Andy was forced to admit just how far his relationship with her had progressed. Somehow she'd become a necessity—the hub of his existence. And while he despised himself for getting into such a mess again, he simply didn't have the energy to do what he'd have to do to reestablish the norm.

Instead he wangled a promise from Honey that she would drop by for dessert after her family left on Thanksgiving. He claimed he wanted her to meet Laney, who hadn't reconciled with her fiancé and would be in town. He and Laney often spent this holiday together; their parents had died years ago and they had just each other. Unfortunately, the two of them were so much alike that they could only cohabit for a day or two before they locked horns.

* * *

"My God, you've grown a foot!" Laney exclaimed when she first laid eyes on Andy upon her arrival at his house Wednesday night.

He laughed at the old joke—one of their grandparents had *always* said that—and moved forward to embrace his kid sister, who wasn't a kid at all, but an attractive young woman.

"So how's tricks?" he asked as he hugged her.

"Let's not talk about me," she replied with a dry laugh, releasing him to retrieve an overnight bag from the car. "Let's talk about *you* and the librarian you've been dating."

Andy blinked in surprise and followed her into the living room, where she rid herself of her bag, purse and jacket. "I'm not dating anyone."

"That's not what I hear."

"What do you hear, and who said it?" Andy instantly demanded, taking the jacket she handed him.

"Susannah Austin wrote me that she'd heard you and a woman named Honey were engaged."

"Su—*Jack's mother?*"

"Of course Jack's mother. You know we correspond."

He didn't, actually, though he should've guessed it. Though Jack and Laney, old friends, had their ups and downs, his mother and Laney had always gotten along well.

"She told me that she hadn't seen anything in the *Winterhaven Daily* yet, but expected to any day."

"Well, tell her not to hold her breath," Andy muttered, plopping down on his recliner. "There's no engagement now, nor will there be one in the future. Honey and I are just friends."

Laney moved to sit on the couch and reached for Andy's remote control instead of replying.

"We really are," Andy repeated. "She has a cute little kid I coach, and we're both working at the library, but that's all."

Laney flipped through the channels.

"She *is* coming over Thursday night to meet you, but not because we're involved or anything. I just thought—"

"Andy?"

"You two would like each other."

"An-dy..."

"I just got rid of one wife. Why in the hell would I want another?"

"Yo, Bro!"

Andy halted his tirade. "What?"

"May I give you a word of advice here?" she asked, leaning over to look him dead in the eye.

"Uh, sure."

"Don't protest so much. It makes you look guilty." Yawning loudly, Laney threw her arms up in a big stretch, then flopped over sideways on the couch. "Am I sleeping on this tonight?" Since Andy and Jaclyn had divided up their furniture when she'd left him, there had been times when a Hide-A-Bed was all he had to offer Laney besides Sarajane's crib.

"No," Andy retorted with a grin. God, but he was glad to have someone in the house with him. "I bought a water bed for the guest room."

She sat up straight, eyes wide. "You did?"

"I did."

"Oh, I do love you!" Laney exclaimed, throwing her arms around his neck. "Even if you're lying about your lady."

Chapter Six

Though Honey enjoyed the holiday visit with her parents and brother, she felt a rush of relief when they finally drove away from her newly rented house around three o'clock that Thanksgiving Day afternoon. She'd slept in a spacious new bedroom last night and in her own bed, thanks to their hard work and Skip's truck. Better yet, she'd managed the move from the trailer before the first of December and so wouldn't have to pay a whole other month's rent.

Congratulating herself that she'd actually spent three days with her mother without their fighting, Honey stepped back into her living room and ran smack into her son. "Oops!" she exclaimed, then laughed.

Wearing a Windbreaker and holding out hers, he looked ready to go somewhere. Honey had a darned good idea where, too.

"My goodness," she teased. "Do we have someplace to go?"

Travis nodded. "Coach Fulbright's to eat punkin pie." For all his adult vocabulary, he could still come through with a child-size error now and then.

"Pu*mp*kin." Honey corrected him out of habit more than anything else and instantly regretted it. They weren't living with Charlie's mother anymore. Travis could be a kid if he wanted. She smiled affectionately at her son. "Surely you're not hungry after all that turkey and dressing you ate at lunch."

"For pumpkin pie, I am."

"I love *punkin* pie myself," Honey replied, and then laughed when he grinned up at her. She slipped into her jacket and followed her son to the porch where he waited with obvious impatience. Minutes later found them in her car en route to Andy's house.

Honey felt as nervous about meeting Andy's sister, Laney, as she was pleased that Andy wanted her to. She wished she'd had the nerve to introduce him to her family, but hadn't dared since her parents were so pro Charlie and con her move to Alabama. Her divorce had shocked them and definitely strained relations. They would never understand her friendship with Andy. But for all that, she'd been glad to see them and most appreciative of the help they'd so willingly offered during the week.

Travis opened the car door before the wheels stopped rolling as she pulled into Andy's drive—something he knew better than to do. He leaped from the car and raced to the front door, where a young woman—probably Laney—met him. She held back the door so he could duck inside, then stepped out onto the porch to wait for Honey to get out of the car.

"You must be Honey Truman."

"Yes," Honey said, openly admiring the woman's shimmering hair and flashing dark eyes. "And you must be Laney."

"The one and only." She smiled Andy's smile. "I'm so glad you're here. Andy's been raving about you all day, and I'd almost decided you were too perfect to be real."

He'd raved about her? "Oh, I'm far from perfect," Honey murmured, joining her on the porch and then preceding her into the house.

Laney laughed as she followed. "Not according to my big brother."

"Not *what* according to me?" Andy asked, walking from the kitchen with Travis at his heels.

"Far from perfect," Laney told him. "I was just telling Honey here how you've raved about her all morning."

"Did I do that?" He looked a bit disconcerted.

"You know you did."

"Yeah, well, Honey has been really good about loaning Travis to me. I give them both full credit for pulling me out of my funk over Sarajane." He smiled down at Travis, standing, as always, at his elbow. "Ready for your pie?"

"Yeah!"

"What about you two ladies? May I serve you some delicious, homemade pumpkin pie?"

"I'm going to pass. I'm still too full from lunch," Laney said, walking over to sit on a corduroy couch in the tastefully furnished living room.

"I'll have a very small piece," Honey told Andy. She moved to help him get it, but he waved her back. "I'll bring yours to you. Visit with Laney. She's leaving in about an hour...unless Jack gets home from deer hunting, that is. She was really hoping to see him since it's been almost a year since last time."

"Okay, but Travis has to eat his in the kitchen," Honey said, eyeing the plush cream-colored carpet that would never be the same if her son ate in the living room.

Andy nodded and vanished into the kitchen.

"You've really worked a miracle on my brother," Laney said once Honey had settled herself on the other end of the long couch. "I haven't seen him this happy in ages."

"He's done a lot for Travis and me, too," Honey replied, covertly inspecting what she could see of Andy's house. She liked it—from the almond-colored walls, to the bay window, to the French doors. "Since my divorce, my son has been without any male influence. I'm very grateful to Andy for providing him a strong role model."

"Andy helps you—you help him.... Maybe the two of you should get married," Laney commented somewhat dryly. "Many's the couple who've united for a more foolish reason—" she sighed and shook her head "—namely, love."

"Can you tell that my sister just broke up with her fiancé?" Andy asked, walking back into the room and holding a plate in each hand. He handed one to Honey before sitting down in his recliner.

"I'm sorry," Laney said with a sigh. "I shouldn't be so negative."

"It's okay," Honey assured her. "Andy and I have already had this very conversation, and we both agree with you. Love shouldn't have any bearing on one's choice of mate."

"You two really talked about this?" Wide-eyed, she looked from one to the other of them. "And you agree with me?"

"Oh, absolutely," Honey said. She then began to eat her pie, which was delicious.

They ate in silence for a moment. When they talked again, it was about other things—Laney's less-than-wonderful job, Andy's half-finished fireplace and Honey's new home which was just too good to be true. At that point, Travis joined them and, at Laney's prompting, began reciting a Christmas list he'd obviously been compiling for some time.

Andy smiled to himself as he listened to the boy. Christmas was nothing without a child around. Thank goodness his own would be home for this year's holiday. He planned to put up a huge tree—probably in that corner over there—and decorate the mantel with evergreens and candles. They would shop for presents, and then the four of them would—

Four of them? Andy's fantasy of family togetherness screeched to a halt. He couldn't believe he'd unconsciously included Honey and Travis in it, and immediately decided that Laney's talk of sensible marriages was the reason why. Marriage to Honey might be sensible...*might be*...but it would never be wise. Marriage had a way of changing people and not always for the good of the union.

Nonetheless, thoughts of being married to Honey continued to haunt Andy after Laney, Honey and Travis left that afternoon and long into the night. Dawn on Friday found him still thinking about her. He didn't wonder why. Marrying men like him were an easy target for misery when they weren't bound to a woman by golden rings and 'til-death-do-us-part.

He missed the camaraderie of marriage; he missed the compromises. He missed Christmas kisses, stolen from an unsuspecting wife under the mistletoe. And though he'd known Honey for only a matter of weeks, he knew instinctively that he could do much worse than hook up with the likes of her.

Had she been totally honest in their conversations about marriage? he suddenly wondered. Could she... would she... really marry someone she didn't love? And if she could and would, what about Andy Fulbright? Could he put his forever where his mouth was?

"Honey, we need to talk."

A picture of beauty in her indigo sweater and jeans, Honey looked out her front door and smiled at Andy as though he dropped by her house every afternoon when she wasn't working at the library. "Okay. May I get this letter finished first, though? I want to get it in the mail before it gets picked up at two o'clock."

"Take your time, take your time," Andy replied, stepping into her living room. She headed down the hall toward the bedroom. He looked around the living room, noting with approval how quickly she had turned her rented house into a home for her and Travis. He saw the couch that matched her love seat, several tables and a piano. Photographs adorned the walls, throw rugs, the floor.

Andy glanced impatiently at his watch. One forty-five. Surely she'd have that letter finished in a minute. Now that he'd realized he had the guts to propose, he was ready to get the show on the road. Not that he intended to pop the question right now. Andy knew Honey would be surprised—well, maybe *shocked* was a better word—by his decision so he planned to give her ample opportunity to get used to the idea. They'd take this thing slow. Very slow...

"Let me put this letter in the box, then I'm all yours." Honey's laughing words shimmied down Andy's spine and lodged somewhere below the belt. She slipped out onto the porch. He heard the rattle of the box. She stepped back into the room. "There, all done."

"Good. Come here."

She gave him a what-are-you-up-to sort of look, but did as requested, joining him where he stood in the middle of the room. "Is something wrong?"

"Nothing's wrong. I want us to go out tonight. Just you and me," Andy said, getting right to the point.

Honey stared at him in silence for a moment. "You mean a...date?"

"A date. Know any baby-sitters?"

"Romy might be available."

"Call her...please."

Honey considered his plea for a second, then shrugged. "She's shopping with Nicole in Birmingham. Travis is with them. I'll ask when Nicole drops him by this afternoon, if that's soon enough for an answer."

"Soon enough," Andy said, moving toward the front door.

"You're leaving already?"

He nodded. "Unlike some people in this town, *I'm* working this Friday."

Honey said not another word until he stepped out onto the porch. Then she called out, "Are you sure about this date thing?"

"Oh, yeah," he affirmed.

"Was that all you wanted to speak to me about?"

"For now."

"For...now," she repeated with an audible gulp that told Andy his decision to take things slow was a good one. Obviously she hadn't experienced a simultaneous, parallel emotional evolution.

Turning on his heel, Andy walked to his truck and drove back to the library, where he worked alone today. Whistling, he labored until the phone rang several hours later. As expected, it was Honey, and she told him Romy was thrilled by the opportunity to earn some extra Christmas shopping money. Andy volunteered to get her on his way to pick up Honey.

Promptly at seven-thirty that evening he did just that. Romy chattered nonstop all the way to Honey's house, words that Andy barely heard until she asked, "Are you going to marry Honey?"

"What?"

"Are you going to marry Honey?" she repeated without batting an eye.

"What makes you wonder a thing like that?" Andy asked.

"Well, you did ask her out on a date," Romy replied with a toss of her silky blond hair.

"Our very first."

"So you're not going to marry her?"

"Why all this preoccupation with weddings?" Andy asked instead of answering her.

"I just think they're neat," Romy told him with a starry-eyed sigh, then added, "Dad's is tomorrow night, you know."

"I know." And he suddenly understood why they were on the teenager's mind.

"I'm the bridesmaid. I have an awesome dress."

"I didn't drag you away from rehearsal, did I?" Andy asked, reaching over to playfully tug her curls.

"No. It's going to be a real small wedding...not at all like the one I'm going to have when I get married."

Hold on to your wallet, Ethan, Andy thought and grinned. He started to ask Romy if she had a beau yet, but didn't since they were now at Honey's house, and he could see Travis already bounding out the door to greet them.

The boy loved Romy, so Andy and Honey had no trouble slipping away. Andy marveled that he felt so awkward around her tonight. It wasn't as though they hadn't spent time alone. They had... at work. But she'd never worn this green silk dress before or those gold earrings, just as he'd never worn these pants or this suede jacket.

First they ate at the town's nicest restaurant, which served Italian food. Over the meal, Andy relaxed until he felt the way he usually felt when around Honey—mentally stunned, sexually aroused.

After eating, they scouted out Winterhaven's two movie houses. The one more popular with the teens of the town boasted three screens and a choice of science fiction, horror or comedy. Since Andy knew from experience that it also boasted floors sticky with spilled soda pop and gum, he drove right by it to the town's older theater, which tonight featured a relatively older movie, *Moonstruck*, but no teenagers. Honey admitted she actually owned the movie, but assured him she didn't mind seeing it again. She loved watching romance and—she didn't verbalize this—could definitely sympathize with the lovesick, spellbound characters in the film.

As the film progressed, Andy decided he loved watching romance, too, especially if he was sitting by a woman who held his hand and cried at the end the way Honey did. Sensing her maudlin mood as the credits rolled,

Andy suggested they go for a drive in the nearby mountains before they returned to her house. Honey agreed with a pleased smile.

Andy loved the mountains and knew them well. For that reason, he drove straight to a lookout popular by day, but always deserted at night. By mutual, unspoken agreement, they braved the chilly air by getting out of the truck and walking to a huge boulder that overlooked the valley that was Winterhaven.

Andy sat down first and leaned back against another rock, spreading his legs so Honey could sit between them, her back resting on his chest. She shivered. He wrapped his arms around her as protection against the breeze.

"Gorgeous, isn't it?" Honey murmured, her gaze on the twinkling panorama below.

"Uh-huh," Andy agreed, not referring to Winterhaven. It was Honey Truman who was gorgeous tonight, and he couldn't resist inhaling the scent of her. To his delight, she tipped her head to one side, allowing him access to her neck. No fool, Andy took what she offered . . . and begged for more by tightening his embrace.

Honey sighed. Andy's blood pressure soared.

She wiggled back even closer against him. He shifted position to accommodate her. Instantly his pants stretched tight over the physical result of their new closeness. Andy squirmed slightly to relieve the pinch.

"You're not comfortable, are you?" Honey asked. Before Andy could protest, she stood and turned to face him. "Is that rock hurting your back?"

"My back's fine," Andy said.

"Your butt, then? This rock is awfully hard."

"My butt's fine, and for your information this rock isn't hard at all compared to certain parts of my anatomy." The words seemed to come of their own volition, rolling off his tongue before he could stop them. Andy tensed, wishing them back.

But Honey just laughed and, to his astonishment, reached out to trace his protruding fly with her forefinger as though his admission came as no surprise. "Just so you know... I want you, too."

That was all Andy needed to hear. Reaching out, he pulled her back into his arms and onto his lap. She cooperated by turning her body and face toward him to initiate a kiss that further fueled his desire.

Andy groaned. Honey laughed again and pressed her lips to his Adam's apple. She then undid the top button of his shirt and pushed the fabric aside so that she could press her lips to the flesh just under his collarbone.

Andy's pulse went berserk. With a low growl, he framed her face in his hands, raising her gaze to his. He kissed her then... deeply, passionately... putting all his need into it. Honey returned the kiss in kind, melting against him, clinging as though weak with wanting.

He moved his hands boldly over her dress, cupping first one breast and then the other with eager fingers. She pressed her upper body closer, a move that twisted and raised her skirt, revealing a length of shapely leg. Fascinated by the sight, Andy pushed the gossamer fabric up to her waist and then fingered the lacy garters he'd uncovered. Honey gasped in response, tipping her head back to kiss his chin and cheek. Andy captured her lips with his and plunged his tongue into her mouth.

They kissed again and again, feverishly, each needing more. He let his hands roam at will, braver with every passing moment since she did not stop his exploration, but actually encouraged it by subtly shifting position yet again to allow him better access to her breasts, now bared, and her hips. Only when he dipped his fingers into the waistband of her panties did she tense ever so slightly.

"Far enough?" he whispered.

She laughed nervously and sat back, pulling down her skirt, rearranging her bra and the bodice of her dress. "Apparently. I honestly thought I was ready for this, but when you—" She hesitated. "W-when you—"

"No explanation necessary," Andy interjected softly. "We are... we have... I mean..."

Honey laughed with real humor now. "Are you telling me I'm not the only one winging this?"

Andy joined in her laughter. "Trust me, honey. You're *not* the only one winging this."

"That sounded like honey with a little *h*."

"It was. You're a real honey and I—" Just in time he halted, saving himself from a thoughtless admission of love that was not the truth, but the result of the moon, the stars and the sexy woman in his arms.

"You what?" Honey asked.

"Want to make love to you."

She laughed again, this time somewhat dryly. "You mean have sex with me, don't you?"

"Uh, yeah, I guess I do." He cleared his throat. "Do you mind the distinction?"

"I'm grateful for it," Honey assured him. "You know how I feel about love."

"So can we? Have sex tonight, I mean?" He tried to pull her close again, but she resisted and looked at his watch, which glowed the time.

"Not unless we can do it in, hmm, five minutes."

"I can. I can," he replied.

"Well, I can't," she retorted, standing. "So we're going to have to save this for another time, another place. What are you doing tomorrow night?"

"I'm going to a wedding," Andy said, standing, too. "And I'm thinking you are, as well."

"Oh, my gosh, I'd actually forgotten! Can you believe it?"

"We could always get together after the ceremony...." he suggested, placing a quick kiss on her mouth.

"Wrong. I'm keeping Romy and Kyle while the bride and groom honeymoon. Nicole's been such a help to me, it was the least I could do."

"True." He rubbed his chin, pretending to think, when in actuality he did nothing more than cherish the view of Honey, bathed in moonlight and hot for him. A heady combination, that. "Sex on a Sunday doesn't seem exactly right, and Monday it's back to business as usual."

"Yeah," Honey agreed somewhat glumly. She rested her cheek on his thudding heart for a moment, then raised her gaze to him. "The cool-down time might not be so bad, you know. Our getting involved sexually is a pretty big step."

And a little out of order with Andy's plans. Not that sex with Honey wasn't in them. It was. *After* their wedding. But she didn't know about that wedding yet, and he didn't think now was the time to tell her.

"We may be rushing things a little for sure," he said accordingly, then added, "You told Romy we'd be back by eleven?"

"I did."

"We have fifteen minutes to get you home."

"Can you do it?"

"I can do it," Andy promised, and then did.

* * *

He didn't see Honey again until the wedding, but thought about her all his waking—and some sleeping—moments.

For that reason, she was a sight for sore eyes when he spotted her and her son at the opposite side of the room in the Winter House where the wedding was to take place. Andy didn't try to sit by her. There were no chairs where she and Travis sat, and he didn't want to lose his own since they seemed a bit scarce. From the looks of things, Ethan and Nicole's small wedding had grown slightly.

Did Romy really want a bigger one than *this?* Andy grinned maliciously at the thought until he remembered he had a daughter, too, who would one day want to wed and expect him to foot the bill.

The ceremony went off without a hitch...except the intended one, of course. When Andy saw Ethan kiss his blushing bride, his heart ached and *not* with pity for his old friend. If anything, he envied Ethan his happiness, an astonishing turnaround he knew he could credit to Honey.

He glanced in her direction to find her watching him instead of the bride and groom. They exchanged a smile. She wiped a tear from her eye and looked away. Maybe I'll pop the question today, Andy thought. Maybe now.

Without any trouble, he found Honey in the ballroom.

"Wasn't it beautiful?" she asked, taking his hand and pulling him over to the wall where she stood. Andy could see Travis playing with Kyle in a corner of the room, well away from the artfully decorated tables spread with all sorts of food and, of course, the bride's and groom's cakes.

"Very nice," Andy replied. "Just the kind of wedding I'd want...and speaking of which, will you marry me?"

Dead silence followed his not-so-brilliantly worded proposal. Then Honey bubbled with laughter. "You won't believe what I thought you said."

"Was it, 'Will you marry me?'" he asked, looking her straight in the eye.

"Ye-es...it...was." Her green eyes rounded in shock. "Oh, my God. You're really asking me, aren't you?" Honey dropped his hand.

"I'm really asking. I know this is sudden, but—"

"Sudden?" She laughed without humor. "I'd say so, yes. The last topic of conversation I remember is the one we had about having sex. We weren't too sure that was the thing to do, as I recall, and now you're proposing?"

"Well, it would solve the sex dilemma," Andy calmly observed. "I mean, if we did get married, the sex would be legal...expected, even."

"Oh, Andy." She shook her head, then laughed, this time with honest mirth. "Needless to say, I'll have to think about this."

"You can't say yes now?"

"No, I can't say yes now."

"Why not?" Andy asked, leaning forward to brush her lips with a kiss.

She sagged against the wall as though her knees had given way. "Because...because..." Suddenly her face lit up. "Because Ethan and Nicole are here, and I want to be the first to hug them." On that note, Honey left him and joined the bride and groom just entering the room.

Ethan had ditched his tie somewhere between the photographs and the reception, but Nicole didn't seem to mind. In fact, Andy thought he saw the tip of it peeking out of the pocket of the cream-colored lace jacket she wore. Romy, dressed in green velvet, followed them into the room but immediately joined some girls her age, who exclaimed loudly over her dress.

Andy started toward Ethan and Nicole to give them his own best wishes, only to be waylaid by Jack.

"So there you are. Mother and I have been looking all over for you."

"I wondered where you were, too," Andy replied as he reached out to hug Jack's mother, Susannah, whom he hadn't seen for several weeks. "Nice wedding, huh?"

Jack gaped at him. "Did you say 'Nice wedding'?"

"Mmm-hmm," Andy absently replied, his gaze on Honey.

"Holy sh—"

"Jack!" Susannah cautioned with an elbow to her son's ribs.

"Shenanigans!" Jack amended. "Not you, too."

"Me what?" Andy asked, meeting his probing gaze squarely on.

"You're going to be next, aren't you?" Jack demanded.

"What are you talking about?"

"Getting married. You and Honey are going to be next, aren't you?" When Andy didn't immediately respond, Jack threw his arms up in utter disgust. "I don't believe it. I stand alone. The last of the die-hard bachelors."

"Is it true?" Susannah, all smiles, asked Andy. "Are you and Honey really engaged?"

"Unfortunately, no," Andy said, a reply that produced a groan from Jack.

"But I wouldn't be wasting my time if I watched the *Daily* for an announcement?" Susannah persisted.

"Well, I—"

"Andy! Come over here." The voice belonged to Ethan, now standing alone, and he motioned for his friend to join him.

Grateful for the chance to escape, Andy murmured, "Excuse me," and slipped away from Jack and his mother. "Congratulations," he said to Ethan, extending his hand. Ethan shook it and added a hug that embarrassed neither.

"Thanks."

When he said nothing else, Andy arched an eyebrow. "Did you need me for something?"

Ethan laughed. "Not really. You were a little red in the face, and knowing how nosy Susannah can be, I figured you might need an out."

"You got that right," Andy muttered with a wry grin. He followed Ethan's gaze to the buffet, where Nicole and Honey now stood. "She's beautiful, isn't she?" he asked, his eye on Honey.

"Yeah," Ethan replied, his eye on Nicole. The men shared a laugh of perfect understanding, and with one exchange of looks, Andy silently thanked Ethan for not asking any questions. At that moment, the women walked back.

"I was just showing Honey what not to eat," Nicole said. "There are boiled shrimp in the cheese balls and fried shrimp in the seafood croquettes."

"I'm allergic, remember?" Honey said when Andy gave her a baffled look.

"Oh, yeah." He turned to Nicole. "May I kiss the bride?"

"Of course," she replied, turning a cheek to accept the caress.

"I'm very glad for you both," Andy then said. "I envy you your happiness."

"There's someone out there for you, too, bud," Ethan said, words that brought an attractive blush to Honey's cheeks. If Nicole noticed it, she didn't let on, and neither did her new husband.

"The kids' bags are by the back door," Ethan said to Honey, "assuming you're still willing to keep them."

"You know I am."

At that moment, Nicole's mother, whom Andy had met once before, walked up to usher her daughter and son-in-law away for the traditional cutting of the cake. Honey moved in that direction with the rest of the crowd. Andy, however, edged back and watched everything from a distance.

Honey didn't even realize this until she felt the weight of a stare and turned to find him clear across the room, watching her. He nodded when their gazes met. She looked quickly away, feeling awkward and embarrassed.

Darn the man for proposing, she thought. Why, it had taken all the nerve she had and then some to agree to an affair. If the moon hadn't been so bright, the sky so full of stars, and Andy so obviously hot for her, she probably would never have even considered it. But she had…and learned Andy wanted the same…so there was no going back.

And now he said that wasn't enough. Now he wanted—she gulped—marriage. Good gravy.

"Mom." Travis, who'd appeared from nowhere, tugged on her dress. "I'm hungry."

Honey looked down at him and smiled. There were many bad reasons to marry Andy, she suddenly realized—financial security, safe sex and companionship among them. But there was really only one good one—

Travis. Glimpsing in her young son's face the man he could become—she realized that that one good reason might be enough to make her tie the knot. Andy was a good man, the kind she wanted her child to be some day.

"Mom..."

"Okay, okay." Honey picked up a plate for Travis and helped him select his favorite foods. Once she'd settled him on one of the chairs lining the room, she went back and filled her own plate with fried drummies, a favorite of hers, fresh-baked rolls, fruit and cheese. She then walked back to Travis and sat next to him.

Out of the corner of her eye, she kept tabs on Andy, who was never alone. In spite of the rumors she knew had circulated after that little fiasco with Marcie, one young woman after another seemed to gravitate toward the carpenter.

Clearly they knew a good catch when they saw one. Why, there probably wasn't a woman in the place who would turn down a proposal from Andy Fulbright, she decided as she nibbled on a third drummie. Why on earth should the likes of Honorine Truman?

At that moment, Andy glanced her way. Honey thought he smiled at her but couldn't be sure since her vision suddenly blurred. She blinked, assuming her contact lens had floated to one side, but the action didn't help.

"Travis, honey, can you see my contact?" Honey asked, turning to her son, who, on more than one occasion, had helped her out of this quandary. He set aside his now-empty plate, stood and peered directly in her eye.

"No."

Honey blinked again, then again. But instead of getting better, her vision actually worsened and a wave of nausea engulfed her.

"Mom?" Travis sounded worried, a sure sign she looked as bad as she suddenly felt.

"I'm okay," Honey told him, adding a weak smile as reassurance. "I'm going to the bathroom for a minute." A splash of cold water would feel so good on her face, which felt flushed. "Stay put, all right?"

"I want to go with you," Travis replied, clearly frightened. And why shouldn't he be? Honey realized. He had no one he could count on but her... no one.

With a nod, she set aside her plate, took his hand and stood. Honey took a stumbling step through the door out into the hall, which abruptly tilted and spun. Feeling deathly ill, she put her free hand on the wall to steady herself.

"Go... get... Andy," she instructed her son even as her knees gave way and the world faded to black.

Chapter Seven

Andy caught Honey before she hit the floor, thanks to the fact that he'd had his eye on her all evening and seen her stumble from the room. Travis helped, too, and though his valiant effort to catch his mother could never have been successful—he just didn't have the size—he did delay her fall, giving Andy the extra seconds he needed to burst into the hall.

"What's wrong with her?" Andy demanded of Travis as he lifted Honey into his arms. He headed away from the wedding reception to a lounge area, where he laid her on a couch. Dropping down on one knee, he brushed her hair back from her face with a hand that trembled.

Travis, wide-eyed and visibly frightened, could only shake his head in reply. At once, Andy's stomach knotted with fear.

"I'm calling 911," he said, standing. He took one step toward the phone, only to halt when Honey touched his wrist.

"Don't," she said. "I-I'm okay, just dizzy. I just need...my medicine." It was obvious that she was struggling to keep her eyes open.

In a flash, both Travis and Andy bent close to her face again. "What medicine? What's wrong?" Andy demanded. Without waiting for a reply, he muttered, "To hell with this. I'm calling an ambulance."

"No, you're not." Honey caught his wrist as though to be sure, then gave a shaky smile probably meant to make him relax. "This is nothing more than an allergy attack. Get my medicine, Travis. You know where it is."

Her son obeyed, dashing out of the room. In a heartbeat, he returned with her clutch bag, from which he extracted a tiny bottle—or tried to. His little hands shook so badly that Andy finally took the bottle from him. He read the label as he twisted the cap, noting that it was a drug commonly prescribed for allergic reactions. "How many of these do you take?"

"Better give me two," Honey said, her voice just slurred enough to scare the wits out of him.

"Travis, get some water out of the bathroom there," Andy ordered at once, pointing to a nearby door.

"She doesn't need it," Travis told him, a statement proved true when Honey took the pills from Andy, raised her head up from the arm of the couch and tossed them into her mouth. She swallowed, then lay back and reached out an arm for Travis, who threw himself across her.

"I take it this has happened before," Andy commented, watching her pat her son's back as though to reassure him.

"Many times," Honey told him without opening her eyes. "Eating out is always tricky for me."

"The shrimp?" Surely she hadn't eaten the seafood after Nicole had taken such care to warn her about it.

"No. All I ate was fruit, a roll, drummies—"

"Drummies? You mean those fried-chicken-wing things?"

She nodded.

"Hell, Honey, they were probably fried in the same oil as the seafood croquettes."

Her eyes flew open. She shook her head in obvious disgust. "Sometimes I think I have soup for brains." She grinned then, impishly, and finally Andy began to relax.

"Well, I wish it'd been soup you ate. Can't you take shots or something for this kind of allergy?" He reached back to scout up a chair so he could sit close by and watch her.

"'Or something,'" she replied. "And I just took it."

"How fast does it work?"

"I'll be good as new—well, better, at least—in twenty or thirty minutes."

Andy glanced at his watch, making note of the time. Seeing Honey ill had shaken him. All he could think about was the things they had not done together yet.

The minutes ticked by slowly. Andy knew because he checked his watch at least every thirty seconds. True to Honey's prediction, she seemed to get better with every passing moment. Her face, once flushed crimson, took on a healthier glow. Her eyelids, droopy before, opened and stayed that way without such a struggle. Finally she raised Travis's head from her tummy and sat up. Andy instantly reached out to help.

"Honey, Andy. . . what's wrong? What's happened?" At the sound of Nicole's voice, Andy glanced toward the door to find her and Ethan standing just inside the room.

"Just a little food reaction," Honey replied. "I'm all right now." She stood, then sat back down almost immediately, a sure indication she wasn't out of the woods yet.

"Did you take your medicine?" Nicole demanded, walking into the room. "Do I need to call a doctor?"

"I took my medicine. You don't need to call a doctor," Honey said. "I'm tons better now."

"Are you sure?" Nicole sat beside Honey on the couch and draped an arm over her shoulders in a hug.

"I'm sure. Really. You've seen me do this before. I know that you know how it goes."

Nicole nodded, but looked very unsure. "We'll postpone the honeymoon, of course."

"You'll do nothing of the sort!" Honey exclaimed, clearly outraged. "I'm all right...really...and just to be sure, Andy's staying at my place tonight, *aren't you, Andy?*" Her eyes pleaded with him to say yes.

"That's right," he said. "So you two can hit the road whenever you like. Everything is under control here."

"I don't know..." Ethan began, a protest halted by Honey's outflung hand.

"It's all settled. Romy and Kyle will be fine with us."

"Well, if you're sure..." Nicole didn't sound at all sure herself.

"I'm absolutely positive," Honey said, standing tall. She did look much better to Andy's discerning eye and walked to the door without any problem. "Now why don't we all go back to the party. I need a glass of punch."

Clearly relieved, Nicole and Ethan led the way back to the reception.

"Are you really okay?" Andy whispered to Honey the moment the bride and groom were out of earshot.

"I'm a bit nauseated, which may mean a night in the bathroom," she replied. "But I honestly think I can manage the kids if you'll help."

"You know I will."

"Thanks, Andy."

"Glad to do it," he murmured, taking her elbow and guiding her into the ballroom.

An hour later found them at her house. As Honey had feared, her system revolted against the iodine. She hadn't been home five minutes before she paid the price with a major stomach upset that resulted in much time spent heaving in the bathroom.

Andy, after settling the kids down with one of the rented movies they'd brought along, hovered like an overzealous nurse until Honey begged him to please give her some privacy. She *would* be all right once she was emptied out.

By midnight, things had quieted down. Honey and the kids slept—Honey in her bed, Romy in Travis's bed, the boys in sleeping bags in the living room.

Andy took the couch and had just dozed off when the phone rang. He leaped off the couch, bounded through the dark into the kitchen and snatched the wall phone off the hook. He didn't want anyone to wake up now that they were finally asleep.

"Honorine Truman, please," said a woman with a very Boston accent.

"She's asleep," Andy answered. "I can take a message if you want, or ask her to call you tomorrow."

"What I want is for you to wake her up," the woman replied. "I must speak to her now."

"Who's speaking?" Andy asked, wondering if the woman might be Honey's mother. He hadn't met her. He didn't know what she sounded like, and this could be some sort of emergency as far as he knew.

"Vera Truman, Honorine's ex-mother-in-law. Who is *this?*"

"A—A friend of Honey's," Andy told her, for some reason unwilling to say more. There was something in this woman's tone of voice that put him on the defensive, and he didn't like it.

To Andy's astonishment, Vera Truman snorted in what sounded like disbelief. "I'll just bet you are. Where is my grandson?"

"He's asleep, too. Now do you have a message for Honey or not?" Andy's patience was fading fast.

"You mean Travis is there *in the house* while you two fornicate?" she raved, her voice shrill.

"Lady, you've got ten seconds to tell me what you want," Andy interjected, resenting the slur on Honey and on him.

"I want my grandson, and you can tell that little tart you're living with that she won't get away with stealing him. We'll see her in court, and before we're finished, she's going to rue the day she took on the Trumans."

Stunned by the woman's vehemence, Andy couldn't think of a response and then didn't have to. The phone clicked dead in his ear. Highly disturbed, he set the receiver into the cradle and walked slowly back to the couch, where he sat and stared at nothing for a very long time.

What could this mean? he wondered. Earlier doubts about Honey reluctantly resurfaced—doubts he tried to ignore, but could not. Obviously Vera Truman had called on behalf of her son. That's what her "we" could mean. Had Charlie changed his mind, then? Did he now want Travis back? Or—and Andy's stomach knotted at the possibility—did this mean Honey had lied to him? That she had really taken Travis without Charlie's permission? That the man now lived without his son, as Andy lived without Sarajane, through no fault of his own?

Andy's blood ran cold at the mere idea.

Abruptly he stood and made his way down the dark hallway to Honey's room, fully intending to get some answers. He stopped short at the doorway. Bathed in moonlight, her hair fanned out over her stark white pillowcase, she looked as innocent as an angel. Knowing what she'd suffered that night, Andy simply could not wake her. He turned on his heel and started back to the couch, only to break into a run when the phone rang again. Andy lunged into the kitchen and snatched up the receiver.

"Hello?" he growled, certain it was Vera calling back.

But it was Nicole. "Andy? Nicole here. How's Honey?"

Andy drew in a calming breath. "Honey is fine and so are Romy and Kyle."

"Really?"

"Really. Where are you?"

"In the honeymoon suite of the Hilton. We just got here and had to have an update before we could relax and...well, you know." She laughed and so did Andy.

"Everything is perfect here," he assured her. "So you and Ethan can 'you know' in peace. I do have one question, though. Some woman, a Vera Truman, called all upset about Honey's stealing Travis. She threatened a court battle—"

Nicole groaned, cutting off the questions he wanted to ask. "That's all Honey needs...a court battle over Travis. She—hold on for a minute, okay?"

"Okay."

Andy heard another voice in the background, probably Ethan's, then, "Are you still there?"

"Still here."

"If everything's really okay, I'm going to hang up. Here's the number where we can be reached...." She rattled off a number, which Andy scrawled across the message board near the phone. "Call if you need us. Otherwise we'll see you soon, okay?"

"Okay," he agreed with a sigh and hung up the phone. Now was obviously not the time to question Nicole about Honey. Her honeymoon—and a very impatient groom from the sound of it—beckoned.

Thoughts of honeymoons filled his head. Mere hours ago, he'd wanted one for Honey and himself. Now that he suspected she might have played him for a fool, he wasn't so sure.

But why would she lie? he asked himself, walking back to the couch once more. He lay back and stared at the ceiling as he tried to come up with one single motive for a deception. Almost immediately, a possible reason sprang to mind.

Honey knew Andy's situation—knew how he felt about women who stole children from their fathers. Could it be that she'd lied so he wouldn't think badly of her?

Maybe, he decided, but why did it matter what he thought of her? They could've continued to live their separate lives without any adverse effects on each other. Working relations might've been less than perfect, but they were both professionals and could cope with people they didn't necessarily admire.

Unless...

What if she did admire him? What if she had done what many women in Winterhaven had done: tagged him as a candidate for the perfect husband/father.

Oh, it wasn't anything to be proud of, this being tagged. It had nothing to do with looks or appeal, after all. It was simply a matter of demographics. He owned a home and a truck. He had a good job. He loved kids. He was unattached.

Had Honey, like some other single women he knew, simply set her cap for him? Possibly, he thought. And that would explain why she'd bother to lie about her own situation. She'd wanted his sympathy, and through clever manipulation, had won it. Hell, she'd won more than that, he ruefully acknowledged. He'd as good as handed over his freedom . . . and wasn't she the coy one to leave him dangling as though there was a possibility she wouldn't take it?

Fat chance of that. She'd take it. Oh, yeah, she'd take it. That was the plan, after all, he was certain.

Honey woke up to bright sunshine in her eyes. She lay without moving for long moments, enjoying the warmth on her skin and thinking about Andy.

What a sweetheart he'd been to look after her and the kids last night. And then there was that astonishing proposal she hadn't fully considered. What to do . . . what to do about this man she admired so much.

Admired . . . or loved?

Frowning, Honey carefully assessed her feelings for Andy Fulbright. If she loved him, then marriage was out of the question. Love meant vulnerability and, ultimately, heartache. Experience had taught her that.

Admiration, on the other hand, was healthy in a marriage, and it was admiration that Honey eventually decided summed up her feeling for Andy. He was a good man, and marriage to him would provide her with the things she needed at this stage of her life—companionship, financial support, and sex among them. Marriage to Andy would also benefit Travis by giving him someone to count on if she became incapacitated as had happened last night.

That little scare, more than anything, brought Honey to the conclusion that a wedding was the only way to go. She and Andy could have a good life together. They both knew what to do this time around. She would take care to give as much as she took, providing him with the things he needed, just as he'd do for her.

Smiling at the thought, Honey climbed out of bed to wash her face and comb her hair. After slipping into her robe, she eased down the hall and through the living room with its sleeping boys.

Honey was prepared to find Andy still asleep, too, but he sat alone at the breakfast table. "Well, aren't you the early bird?" she greeted him.

Not only did Andy not crack some joke about breakfast worms as she expected, he didn't even crack a smile. "Feeling better?"

"M-much," she replied somewhat hesitantly. He sounded quite cool and looked rather... what? She simply couldn't read his enigmatic expression.

"Good, because I have a message for you from Vera."

Honey's heart slammed to a halt, then went crazy. "Vera called?"

Andy, his gaze unwavering, nodded. "Last night while you were asleep."

Stunned to her toes by this development, Honey slowly moved to join Andy at the table. "What did Vera want?" she asked, though she could guess. Obviously her ex-mother-in-law had just arrived home from her extended vacation in Italy and now knew that Honey and Travis had moved south.

"She wants Travis. Says she'll see you in court if that's what it takes to get him back." His voice held no emotion.

"Court? Did you say court?" Court that took time? Court that cost money? Court that would put their lives at the mercy of some uncaring judge? "Surely, surely she wouldn't—"

"So it's true. It's all true." Andy's gaze narrowed. "Why did you lie to me about this?"

So agitated was Honey over the news about Vera, Andy's question barely registered. "What?"

"You lied to me. You said you didn't steal Travis from Charlie."

"I said I—" Belatedly the words slammed into her consciousness—*steal Travis from Charlie.* "You think I stole Travis?"

"Well, it's pretty damned obvious, isn't it?" Andy shook his head as if thoroughly disgusted with the likes of her. "I mean, I don't hear you denying it." He leaned back and crossed his arms over his chest, as though waiting for her to make that denial.

"And you won't," Honey snapped, thoroughly disgusted herself and not a little hurt. "I owe you no explanations for anything I may or may not have done before I met you."

Andy, face flushed, came to life—scooting his chair back, standing to tower over her. "So that's how it is."

"That's how it is."

He stared at her for a moment. "I thought you were different. I thought you were special. I...I...God, what an idiot I am." Without another word, he snatched up his jacket, strode to the front door and vanished through it. Only the sound of his truck, roaring to life outside, told Honey what conclusions he must have drawn.

She jumped to her feet and followed. Stepping out onto the porch, she yelled, "Damn you!" to his truck, now heading away down the street. Her words echoed loudly in the chilly morning stillness, and she cringed, hoping she had not awakened anyone in the house or down the street. A quick inspection proved she had not and, fighting tears, Honey walked back to her bedroom, shut the door and sat on the bed.

How could Andy think she'd lied about Travis? she wondered, experiencing again the pain of his betrayal. She'd never been anything but honest, never— On that thought, Honey frowned and gave some thought to the word *honest*. She'd told Andy everything about Charlie and Travis, yes, but how much about Vera?

Very little, actually. But how could Honey admit that she had deliberately arranged to move while Vera was out of the country because Charlie would never have agreed to it otherwise? She'd look devious to Andy—and anyone else, she guessed—when in reality, she'd only done what she had to do.

Charlie didn't care beans about Travis and never had. But his mother—his overbearing, interfering snob of a mother—did. Oh, it wasn't real love... at least not what Honey considered love to be. It was a smothering sort of affection that waxed and waned according to whether or not Travis was a "good boy."

Honey shuddered at the memory of the confrontations—near altercations—she and Vera had had over the raising of her son. Honey despised the woman for the hell she'd put her through. Despised her and felt not one qualm of guilt that she'd moved to Alabama without warning or discussion.

As for Andy...well, she felt no guilt about what she'd told—or hadn't told—him. If he considered her omissions a lie, then so be it. She owed him no explanations, either...especially now. They meant nothing to each other.

Abruptly, tears welled up in Honey's eyes and then spilled over onto her cheeks. Alone in her room with the door closed, she cried over Vera, who wouldn't stay out of her life, and Travis, who would be caught in the middle...again. Not one tear fell for Andy, though, and not one would. Any man so willing to believe the worst was not worth his salt. Thank goodness she'd found out in time.

Honey heard not one word from Andy all that Sunday and was glad for that even though it hurt so much she half suspected she'd lied to herself about what he meant to her.

On Monday, she didn't step out of her office except to visit the rest room and later inform Andy that she would pick up Travis after football since she was taking off early to fetch Romy and Kyle. He did nothing more than grunt in reply, reaffirming the cold hard facts: he wanted nothing more to do with a liar such as she.

Tuesday was pretty much a repeat of Monday, minus the one conversation. Andy stayed on the deck; Honey stayed in her office. They didn't exchange so much as a "Hi, how are you?" Honey told herself she didn't mind. She was well rid of him, she decided. Any man so willing to believe the worst would be hard to live with.

On Wednesday, Nicole and Ethan returned, all smiles and happiness. Though Honey should've been thrilled to see them so content, she actually cried again after they picked up their children and left. She did it out of sight of Travis, of course. He'd begun to wonder aloud about Andy's absence, and she didn't feel up to explaining it.

As for Andy, he moped around his house most nights, lonelier than ever and wishing to hell he'd never met Honey or her son. It was in just such a mood that Ethan found him late Friday night when he made a surprise visit to see if he was still alive and well.

Andy assured him that he was, then invited him in. The two looked at honeymoon photos—Ethan was a shutterbug if ever there was one—and then made awkward conversation since Andy did not seem to be acting very cordially.

"Are you mad at me about something?" Ethan finally demanded in visible frustration.

"No," Andy growled.

Ethan sat in silence for a moment. "I hope this doesn't have anything to do with the honeymoon. I know you had to stay at Honey's to help with the kids—"

"This has nothing to do with you, Ethan," Andy said, suddenly standing. "Want a beer?"

"Sure," Ethan said as he followed him into the kitchen. He waited until Andy handed him an ice-cold can. "So what gives? I can see you're perturbed about something."

"It's nothing—"

"Come on, bud. I can read you like a DC comic. What's up?"

With a sigh, Andy motioned Ethan back to the living room. "It's Honey," he admitted, and then went on to explain what had happened.

"I have to admit I don't know a damned thing about this," Ethan said. "But I can hook you up with someone who does, I'll bet." He reached for the telephone.

Andy clamped his hand on the receiver. "I'm in no mood to talk to Honey tonight."

"I'm not calling your woman," Ethan said, snatching the phone away. "I'm calling mine."

Ethan punched out the number, waited, then smiled, a sure sign Nicole had answered. Andy listened in silence as his friend explained the problem. Ethan paused, did a little listening of his own, then handed the phone to Andy. "She wants to speak to you."

"Great," Andy muttered. "Hello, Nicole."

"Men are such idiots," Nicole responded instead of returning the greeting. "How could you possibly think Honey would lie to you about Charlie or anything else for that matter?"

"Are you saying she told me the truth?"

"Of course I am. I've known Charlie for years. I can vouch for the fact that he never wanted Travis and that he was agreeable to Honey's move to Winterhaven."

"If that's so, why is Vera Truman in such a snit?"

"Because Honey and Travis are no longer under her thumb, I expect," Nicole said. "She never thought Honey was good enough for Charlie. Still doesn't believe she's capable of raising Travis right."

"You know this for sure?" Andy questioned somewhat suspiciously. "Or are you basing this on what Honey's told you?"

"Yes, I'm basing it on what she's told me," Nicole admitted. "But, Andy, I honestly believe it's true. Honey is such a good person. Surely you know that by now."

"I know it...."

"Then what's the problem? Jaclyn?"

Andy sighed. "Probably...or maybe it's just me. You know... once bitten, twice shy?"

"Honey is not Jaclyn."

"No."

"So are you going to call her, or what?"

"Damned if I know." He sighed again.

"Will it help you reach a decision if I tell you she's really down in the dumps about this?"

"She is?"

"She is."

"Then maybe I will call...."

"Thank goodness. Now would you please send Ethan home?"

Andy glanced over at Ethan, waiting so patiently nearby. "Nicole says you've gotta go home now."

Ethan stood immediately. "I'm on my way."

Andy shared that information with Nicole, hung up the phone, and followed Ethan to the door. "Do you always leap when she says frog?"

"Yep," Ethan said.

"I never thought I'd see the day," Andy murmured, shaking his head with feigned bemusement.

"She's got me henpecked for sure."

"And in less than a week," Andy agreed. "What's her secret?"

"The negligees," Ethan said as he stepped out onto the porch.

"The *what?*"

"The negligees. She has a different one for every night of the week, thanks to a shower some of her friends gave her. I've already peeked at tonight's. It's see-through red with these little—"

"Never mind. I don't want to know."

While Ethan laughed at him, Andy stepped back and slammed the door. Alone once more, he grinned, pleased as punch that Ethan had found Nicole and was so obviously happy.

And what about me? he wondered a millisecond later, his smile fading. Was Honey *his* Nicole—that one-in-a-million woman who could make him happy. He wanted to believe it and to believe in her.

I do believe in her.

Andy sucked in a deep breath, then finger combed his hair. He stared at the phone for a second, downright nauseous with uncertainty, trying to find the courage to walk over to it. Sitting down on the couch, he reached for the phone, raised the receiver to his ear and punched out the number.

She answered on the third ring.

"Honey, it's Andy," he said, and was rewarded for his bravery by a soft click and a better-luck-next-time dial tone.

Chapter Eight

"Who was that?" Travis asked, the moment Honey hung up the phone.

"Wrong number," she told him, the truth to her way of thinking. If Andy had called to further insult her, he'd definitely dialed the wrong number. Besides, she didn't want Travis to know about the fight. He'd surely ask the why of it, and Honey didn't know how to explain Andy's betrayal.

Betrayal? Maybe not *that* exactly, but his conclusion-jumping hurt Honey every bit as much. Of course her current misery might not be all his fault, she admitted. Thoughts of a possible court battle over custody of Travis had taken their toll, too. Damn that Charlie for not having the guts to stand up to Vera. He'd always been such a wimp where his mother was concerned—never once supporting Honey when she and Vera had disagreed over how Travis should be raised. He wouldn't this time, either, she knew, which meant his written agreement regarding her move to Alabama would be as worthless as he'd always been.

Monday found Honey almost sick with dread over facing Andy, as she surely must. They'd be working under the same roof, after all. But to her surprise, Andy did not show up for work that morning. At noon, she picked up the phone in her office and called Nicole under the guise of discussing the clerical help she was ready to hire to input data about each cataloged book into the computer.

They agreed that a classified advertisement should be run in the *Winterhaven Daily* as soon as possible. Heavy silence followed their mutual decision while Honey drummed her fingers on the desk top and tried to figure out how to ask a question about Andy without appearing too obvious.

"So tell me," Nicole said before Honey could speak again, "what do you think about Andy's taking a week off from his library work to weatherproof the Widow Klausen's house? You've heard of her, haven't you? She's the woman who lives down by the cemetery. You know, the one who takes in all those foster children and does such a wonderful job raising them?"

Honey stopped drumming. "Is that where Andy is?"

"Yes, the sweetheart. Didn't he tell you?" Nicole sounded surprised.

"No. I haven't talked to him since we...well...in ages."

"I thought he was going to call and apologize Friday night."

That's why he'd called? To apologize? Her stomach knotted with regret that she hadn't given him the chance. "He told you about our, um, misunderstanding?"

"Yes, and I stood up for you, of course. That's when Andy promised to call. I really thought he would, too."

Honey winced. "Actually...he did. I hung up on him."

"Honorine Truman!" Nicole exclaimed. "For shame."

"He called me a liar," Honey retorted.

"Don't you know that was his past talking? Give the man a break."

"Whose side are you on, anyway?"

"Yours and his," Nicole replied. "That's why I want you two to make up. Now, is he going to drop Travis by the library this afternoon?"

"As far as I know."

"Then take some friendly advice from someone who loves you. Be there at the door waiting for him and clear this mess up. You two are worse than Romy, for goodness' sake. Every little misunderstanding is a major crisis with her right now, but she, at least, has puberty to blame."

It was a thoughtful Honey who hung up the phone moments later and a forgiving Honey who ran to the door the moment she heard Andy's truck brake in front of the library after football practice that afternoon. By the time she stepped out onto the porch, her son ran up the walk and the truck rolled away. She did wave, though, and was rewarded by a wave in return. Andy did not brake the truck again, as she'd hoped. Nor did he call that night.

On Tuesday, he waved first. And though he didn't tarry that day, either, he did smile at her through the window. Honey smiled back, hoping to encourage him into calling later. It didn't work. The phone never rang, and Honey couldn't bring herself to call him. This whole screwup was Andy's fault, after all, and while she'd forgive him if he apologized, she'd be damned if she'd beg him to do it.

By Wednesday afternoon, after a long day in a too-quiet library, Honey questioned her decision to wait for Andy to take the initiative. Now that she thought about it—and had she ever thought about it!—he'd already done that: last Friday when he phoned. That meant the ball was in her court.

But it wasn't Andy who dropped Travis off that afternoon. The mother of one of the other players did the honors, explaining that she'd seen Honey's advertisement for a library assistant and wanted to ask a couple of questions about it. A very disappointed Honey answered them and then gave the woman an application to fill out. Her pride in her pocket by then, Honey actually tried to phone Andy around eight o'clock that night, but only got his answering machine. In a heartbeat, she lost her nerve and hung up.

Friday afternoon, when she'd given up on their ever settling this thing, Andy surprised her by hopping out of his truck and striding up the walk to where she stood on the porch. "Are you still angry with me?" he asked by way of greeting the moment Travis disappeared into the house-turned-library to find his waiting snack.

"Not as much as before," Honey admitted, looking him square in the eye. My oh my, what a sight he was in that clingy sweat suit. She'd forgotten just how her hormones loved the maleness of him.

"I should've known better... about you and Charlie, I mean."

She easily shrugged her full forgiveness of what seemed like a very little transgression, thanks, no doubt, to her lonely week plus Nicole's words of wisdom. "You *would've* known better if I'd told you the whole story."

Andy smiled then, an expression that put that familiar old twinkle in his dark blue eyes. "So tell it to me now."

"Not now. Later. After supper, that is, if you can stay...."

His face fell. "I have to work tonight—a project I'm doing on my own time. But how about tomorrow after the game? It's a late one—five o'clock. We are going together, aren't we? Same as usual?"

"Same as usual," Honey said, so relieved to be uttering those words.

Andy left within minutes. Just an hour after that, Honey and Travis drove to their new house, where she found waiting, in her mailbox, a letter from Vera Castorini Truman. Scathing, abrupt, it spoke to a subject near and dear to both their hearts: the future of one five-year-old boy named Travis.

Travis's team won their last game, much to Honey's delight. She was proud of her son and his coach and more than a little disappointed that the peewee football season had ended. Now that she finally understood the sport a little, she actually enjoyed the games, not to mention sitting high in the metal bleachers, snacking and people watching.

The three of them stayed for the next game, too, sitting together like the family they weren't. Andy didn't say too much beyond apologizing again, a fact about which Honey worried until he caught one of her searching glances and held it. She blushed from head to toe—her flesh burning as though he'd run his hands over her.

His eyes promised that they would talk at length. His smile promised peace and a once-and-for-all end to their misunderstanding. Honey released any secret worries in a sigh of pure relief. After a darned stressful week, her life—the Winterhaven part of it, anyway—seemed to be on an even keel again.

After the game, the three of them walked to the parking lot, only to be waylaid by Matt, Travis's friend, and his mother. They wanted Travis to celebrate the end of the football season with a fast-food hamburger. Glad for the chance to talk to Andy alone, Honey agreed. Matt's mother promised to bring him home later.

So it was only Honey and Andy who got into his truck and drove to her house. The moment they stepped through the front door, Andy swept her up into his arms and kissed her as though there were no tomorrow. Or was it yesterday he tried to obliterate? Honey didn't know and didn't care. It just felt too wonderful to be held by him again. Though she wished she could take advantage of Travis's absence to seduce Andy on the couch, Honey soon slipped free of his embrace.

They had to talk first.

As though reading her mind, Andy took Honey's hand and led her to the love seat. Andy sat at one end; Honey nearby. She turned and tucked her legs under her so she could see his face.

"This past week without you has been pure hell," Andy said with a shake of his head. "I can't believe I ever thought you were the kind of woman who'd steal a kid."

"Please don't apologize anymore," Honey replied, placing a finger on his lips. "You made a logical assumption that I've come to realize might not be so far off the mark."

"What are you talking about?"

"This." With some hesitation, Honey handed Andy the letter from Vera.

He stared at the envelope for a moment, then pulled the handwritten letter from it. Anxiously, Honey watched his expression as he scanned the words Vera had written about her grandson—troubling words that had haunted her ever since she'd read them herself.

But his expression never changed. When he'd finished reading, Andy simply refolded the letter, tucked it back into the envelope and handed it to Honey. "So that's what this is all about."

"Yes," Honey said. "Vera thinks I should've waited until she was back in the States before I moved. But how could I? Charlie would never have relinquished his bi-weekly custody rights if she'd said not to. . . even though he hadn't honored them once since she left the country." She paused, scrutinizing Andy's expression, trying to read his mind. He revealed nothing of his thoughts, nor did he speak. "You think I was wrong, don't you? You think I should've considered her feelings."

Andy shrugged by way of reply. "I got a letter today myself," he told her. "From France." Bending his body to the side just a little, Andy dug into the back pocket of his sweatpants and extracted his wallet. From it, he withdrew a color photograph, which he handed to her with a one-word explanation, "Sarajane."

Blond and petite, big blue eyes glowing with mischief, Andy's beautiful daughter laughed at the camera. It was obviously a summer shot. She was standing on a grassy field somewhere, holding a baseball bat poised as though ready to swing. On her riotous curls, its bill rakishly tipped, sat a cap with an Alabama *A* on it even though she lived an ocean away.

For a heartbeat, Honey felt—really felt—Andy's loss. She caught her breath at the intensity of the pain. Her eyes swam with tears—tears for this man, his daughter, and for every other parent or—God forgive her for what she'd done—grandparent who'd experienced such a loss.

"What can I say?" Overcome with guilt, Honey thrust the photograph into his hands and stood... or tried to. To her dismay, Andy reached out and prevented her escape by pulling her into his arms instead. She resisted for half a second, then clung to him, tears streaming down her face. "I've never lost anyone I've loved. I just didn't realize..."

"But you do now," he whispered with as much emotion, holding her tight, stroking her hair. Long moments passed before Honey eased free of his embrace and sat back on her heels again.

"What should I do?"

"Telephone her," Andy replied without hesitation. Standing, he walked to the door.

"Where are you going?" Honey demanded, staring at him in disbelief.

"Home, so you can make that call."

"The hell you are," she retorted, unladylike words that clearly startled him. Honey scrambled off the couch and joined him at the door. "I need you here for moral support, Andy Fulbright."

"Okay, okay." He grumbled the words, but she could tell that he didn't mind and might even be pleased.

Honey led him back to the couch, where she invited him to sit by placing a hand on each of his shoulders and pushing down. He did as commanded, a smile tugging at the corner of his mouth. Sucking in a deep breath, she walked to the kitchen, retrieved the cordless phone and walked back to plop down next to Andy. He draped his left arm across her shoulders at once, a comforting gesture that gave her the courage to punch out the familiar number.

Vera answered on the third ring. "Truman residence."

"Vera? It's Honorine. Do you have a minute? I'd like to talk to you."

"I assume you received my letter today."

"I did—" Honey patted her hammering heart "—and I want to say that I... that you... that, um, Charlie..." Abruptly, Honey raised her hand to cover the mouthpiece, whispered a four-letter word that made Andy choke, then dropped her hand back to her heart. "What I'm trying to say is you're-right-I'm-wrong-and-I'm-sorry." The admission, once past the tip of her tongue, tumbled out so quickly that the words ran together.

"Excuse me?"

"I'm wrong," Honey repeated, noting that the words came more easily the second time. "I'm wrong. I know it now, and I'm so sorry." Silence, most likely of the stunned variety, followed Honey's apology. She glanced at Andy, who immediately gave her a wink and a grin of encouragement. "Vera? Are you still there?"

"I'm... here." Her voice sounded strained. "I... simply... didn't expect you to say this."

"Hmm, well, just for the record, I didn't expect me to say this, either. But I have, and I mean every word. I should never have slipped away as I did."

"You had no right," Vera said.

Honey tensed at the accusation. Reaching up, she found and held on to Andy's hand, which rested on her shoulder. "Actually, I have every right to do as I please with my child. What I meant was, I did you an injustice by moving without at least warning you. I'm not proud of that. It was a cowardly thing to do. I just thought if I could get away from Boston, I could start over. I knew that you'd try to influence Charlie against me."

"You've taken away my son's world."

"*His* world?" Honey asked ever so softly. "Or yours? Charlie was glad to see us leave, Vera. He doesn't want to be a daddy... never has."

"Trumans do not shirk their responsibility."

"Travis should be more than just a responsibility to Charlie. He should be his *pride and joy!*"

Silence followed Honey's passionate exclamation. Then to her astonishment, she heard the sound of what just might be sobbing.

"Vera?"

"I'm still here," came the husky reply.

"Travis and I are so happy in Winterhaven. I have a good job. He's fitting right in at school and has new friends. He's even played football. Please don't do anything to spoil this."

"You let that child play football?" Vera's voice sounded stronger.

"Yes, and he's learned discipline, as well as how to win and lose." Honey glanced at Andy when she quoted those words he'd once said. He smiled encouragingly and gave her a thumbs-up. "Whether or not you want to admit it, Vera, there is more of me in Travis than there is of Charlie. Oh, he's got your son's looks, all right, but his fighting spirit is mine... all mine."

"I have always admired that about you," Vera admitted to Honey's astonishment. "And I agree that Charles is sadly lacking that quality. That's why I push him so, you know. Why, he'd be content to be a mail clerk in a corporate basement somewhere...."

And happier. Honey silently replied.

Abruptly, Vera sighed. "I have a right to see Travis on a regular basis. You know that I do."

"Yes."

"I think one weekend per month isn't too much to ask if I pay for the airline tickets."

Honey's heart began to thud against her rib cage. "Will that be enough time for both you and Charlie to see him?"

"That's Charlie's problem," Vera said. "He gave up his visitation rights to his son all by himself. He can do his own renegotiating."

"Then one weekend a month it is," Honey quickly agreed. In a burst of generosity, she added, "Travis is out of school for over two weeks for Christmas. Would you like him to stay with you a few extra days this month?"

"Yes. Yes, I would. The holidays seem flat without a child around."

Touched by Vera's obviously emotional sentiment, Honey actually found herself blinking back tears of sympathy. "I know. That's why I can't let him go until after Christmas Day. You do understand that, don't you?"

"Yes, of course."

"Shall I call you tomorrow night to work out the details? I'm not sure of the exact date he goes back to school."

"Please," Vera agreed. Moments later, she hung up the phone, but not before the women exchanged a goodbye that was almost cordial.

Honey gave the phone a little toss onto the couch, then turned into Andy's embrace, hugging him hard to show her gratitude for his support.

"What a load off!" she exclaimed, her face buried in his sweatshirt, just about heart-high.

"So everything's going to be all right?"

"Yes. Vera says one visit a month will satisfy her."

"And Charlie?" Andy patted her back rather absently, as though deep in thought about something.

Honey raised her face to mere inches from his. "Neither of us is going to worry about him. If he really wanted to see Travis, he'd call."

Andy digested that in silence, probably struggling to comprehend the possibility that a man wouldn't want to see his son. "Maybe he'll make an effort once Travis gets to Boston."

"Well, I hope Vera doesn't let him in the house. He doesn't deserve to see his son."

Placing his hands on Honey's shoulders, Andy set her back away from him and then stood. He scooped up the cordless phone and walked to the blue-and-yellow kitchen where he replaced it on its wall-mounted base. "Don't you think a little forgiveness might be in order here?"

"Have you forgiven Jaclyn?" Honey retorted by way of reply.

Andy, now leaning negligently against her doorjamb, considered her question for several long moments. "I'm trying. I'm really trying."

At once ashamed of her outburst, Honey sprang from the couch and threw her arms around his waist in a hug of sympathy and perfect understanding. He hugged her back, squeezing so tightly she could barely breathe. Honey didn't mind. She'd never felt this close to him before and didn't want the moment to end.

"Are you going to marry me...or what?" he suddenly asked, shattering the silence.

"Depends on the 'or what,'" Honey sassily replied, her heart singing for joy.

"Cohabitation without the benefit of clergy," Andy replied with the utmost seriousness.

Honey struggled not to laugh. "You can't mean an affair."

"That's exactly what I mean."

"Those two are my only choices?"

"Yep."

"Then I definitely pick marriage."

"Y-e-e-s!" Andy exclaimed, proceeding to impress the heck out of Honey by lifting her up high in the air.

She gasped, then struggled to be put down. "Good grief," she exclaimed, when he set her on her feet again. "My fiancé the muscle man!"

"I lift weights two or three nights a week," Andy explained, raising his arm and flexing his biceps in the classic bodybuilder's pose.

Honey dutifully touched the muscles in question, which were impressively formed. "Ooh! Aah! I had no idea you were so dedicated."

"Dedicated, hell," Andy retorted, lowering his arm. "I work out to keep from staring at the four walls at night."

"When we're married, you'll have much more to do than that. Will you still work out?" Honey grasped a handful of his sweatshirt in each hand and pulled, forcing him to take a step forward so that they stood body-to-body, her eyes level with his chin. She tipped her head back to meet his gaze.

"Every night." He rested his hands on her waist.

"Every night? But that's more working out...not less! Why, you'll have biceps as big as...as—"

"That's not the muscle I plan to exercise," Andy quietly interjected.

"It's not?"

He shook his head.

"Then which..." she teased, even though their proximity made it plain which of his muscles needed the most attention.

"Guess." He kissed her then, the sweetest of kisses that promised so much more. Honey shivered with a sudden, intense desire for him.

"Hold me."

He did, slipping his hand from her waist to mold her hips and lift her to his need. Honey slipped her arms around his neck and shuddered, at once shaky with wanting.

"When can we do this wedding thing?" Andy asked between the kisses he planted on her mouth, cheeks and neck.

"Soon," Honey promised, tipping her head back so she could catch her breath.

"How soon?" he demanded, raising her even higher, turning so that the wall helped support her weight. She helped by wrapping her legs around his waist, then cherished the feel of his mouth pressed to her breast. Her flesh burned as though her blouse and bra were not even there and, in truth, she wished they weren't.

"Very...very...soon," she gasped. "Next month. Next week. Tonight."

Andy groaned. "Not soon enough."

"No."

They kissed again, so lost in the magic that the sound of a car door slamming didn't even register. The stomping of feet on the porch did, however, as did the sound of the doorknob turning. Honey and Andy sprang apart. He vanished into the kitchen. She whirled toward the door just in time to see it fly open and her son walk into the living room.

"Well, hi there," she said, praying that her clothes weren't askew.

"Hi," Travis responded. He glanced around. "Where's Coach?"

"In the kitchen."

Travis headed that way at once. Instead of following, Honey collapsed on the couch and stole a second to recover and regroup.

A wedding. Hers and Andy's.

Honey smiled, relishing the thought of being Mrs. Andy Fulbright, wife of the right man. Theirs would be a good marriage, built on nothing so foolish as love, but on compatibility, compassion and common sense.

A wedding. So much to do...

She wouldn't be ready by tomorrow, of course, no matter how much their hormones begged. But since this was a second ceremony for both of them and would, therefore, be small, she could probably get everything done by the day after Christmas. Then Travis could stay with Vera while she and Andy honeymooned.

A honeymoon. With Andy. Just the two of them...

Honey leaned back, closed her eyes and imagined how wonderful it would be. It was just that way that Andy and Travis found her moments later. Travis leaped onto the couch next to her. "Mom?" He shook her. "Are you asleep?"

"Well, if she was, she isn't now," Andy replied.

Honey opened her eyes and smiled at both. "I'm not asleep. I'm thinking."

"'Bout what?" her son asked.

"Oh, lots of things," Honey replied, glancing up at Andy.

"Second thoughts?" he asked, a question that clearly baffled Travis.

"Not a one," she said.

"You've set a date, then?"

"For what?" Travis asked, looking from one to the other.

Honey ignored him. "How does December 26 sound?"

"For what?" Travis repeated.

Andy ignored him. "We can't do it sooner?"

"I really don't see how."

"Then December 26 it is."

"For what?" Travis as good as shouted.

"For a very special Christmas present," his mother told him, unwilling to share everything just yet. She knew her impatient son well and didn't want to begin every morning until the twenty-sixth with, "Is it today, Mom?" "Now I think it's time you bathed and hit the sack, son."

"But I want to stay with you and Coach," Travis predictably argued.

"Coach has to go home and get his own bath," Andy replied. "But I will stay long enough to tuck you in if you hurry." Having said that, he snatched Travis up off the couch. Carrying him like a bag of potatoes, he then strode down the hall to the bathroom, Travis giggling all the way.

Smiling, Honey watched their antics. A feeling of intense happiness began somewhere in the region of her heart and quickly spread until she felt warm from head to toe.

It's going to happen, she realized. Travis will have a father who loves being one. I will have a husband who wants to be one.

A perfect setup. What more could any woman ask?

The next week flew by, a blur of stolen kisses, secret smiles, whispered plans. Andy found that part of his concentration remained with Honey, making his carpentry work darned difficult. Since Ethan's new wife still occupied his thoughts, most of the business of Do It Right, Inc. fell on Jack's shoulders. And while the electrician was really quite capable—he'd run his former business singlehandedly—Andy was glad for the help of Grady O'Shea and Tim Portland, the men they'd hired to help handle the increased demands for their services. They still needed a full-time bookkeeper, but he intended to supervise the hiring of one the first free moment he found.

Such moments were rare since he now juggled his day job, his soon-to-be wife and stepson and the work required to turn his bachelor pad into living quarters more suited to a family life-style. Specifically Travis needed a suitable bedroom along with a playroom for his toys. Andy had the rooms empty until now, but they needed some remodeling that he was hard-pressed to accomplish. For even though football season had ended, he was spending more of his spare time at Honey's helping Travis make Christmas presents for his mother, father, uncle and grandparents. They labored for hours on the gifts—bluebird boxes fashioned from wood according to the strict specifications these particular feathered friends demanded before they would move in and build their nests.

The two of them worked in the garage, currently off-limits to Honey. Every night for a couple of hours, they sawed, hammered and painted together, making steady progress toward the completion of the birdhouses. Andy would then oversee Travis's bath and tuck him in, at which time he and Honey would exchange a good-night that took anywhere from thirty minutes to an hour and involved lots of hot kisses and urgent touching.

He always left in a terrible state—heart hammering, body tense with unrequited passion—and so counted off the time left until the wedding by marking a big black X on each day on the calendar. He could've saved himself a lot of frustration, of course, by limiting the good-night to one short kiss.

But to Andy's way of thinking, their sampling of the pleasures to come was worth the price he paid in physical misery. Honey had made it clear that her sexual appetite equaled his. Andy appreciated that honesty and longed for the day when the two of them would finally be truly alone together to begin their lifetime experimentation in pleasing one another.

Chapter Nine

Bright and early on the morning of Saturday, December twelfth, Andy sat in Honey's kitchen, eating a breakfast of pecan waffles, maple syrup and link sausages. A day's worth of tasks lay ahead of them, waiting to be accomplished. First on the list: telling Travis about the wedding.

Oddly nervous about it, Andy waited for Honey to do the honors. If her technique proved a good one, he intended to copy it December 22, when he met Sarajane's plane. Since this was not the sort of announcement a father made over the phone, he couldn't tell his daughter earlier, though he had begun to talk about Honey and Travis to let Sarajane become acquainted with their names. Andy figured that while in the Big Apple, he and Sarajane would shop for a dress she could wear to the wedding.

"Travis," Honey said as she set his plate in front of him, "I have a surprise for you . . . a sort of early Christmas present." She glanced over to Andy, obviously nervous.

Travis, as though picking up on their vibes, looked from one to the other. "What is it?"

Honey placed one hand on the back of his chair, the other on the table and squatted so that their eyes met. "Coach Fulbright and I are getting married. He's going to be my husband and your stepdad."

Though Andy wasn't sure exactly what kind of reaction he'd expected, it wasn't the solemn nod that Travis now gave them. Unsure of what that meant, Andy looked at Honey, who looked back at him, and shrugged equal bewilderment.

"Are you surprised?" she asked Travis.

"Uh-uh," he coolly replied around a bite of waffle. Travis had long since dispensed with the more formal "No, ma'am" always required by Vera.

"You mean you knew we were getting married?" Andy asked, unable to stay out of the conversation any longer.

"Uh-huh," the boy told him.

Honey and Andy exchanged another glance. "But how did you know?" she demanded of her son.

"Santa told me."

"Santa?" Honey frowned. "When did you see Santa?"

"When Nicole and Romy and Kyle and me went to Birmin'ham."

"I'd forgotten you saw him that day," Honey murmured thoughtfully. "And he actually told you that Andy and I would be getting married?"

Travis shrugged. "Sorta. That's what I asked him for, and I've been good... well, pretty good." He grinned mischievously at his mom, who'd just arched an eyebrow at him.

"That's debatable at times, but overall, yes, you have been good," she teased, planting a kiss on the top of his head. Standing to her full height, she walked around to seat herself at the table. "That's not really why Andy and I are getting married, though."

"It's not?"

"No," Andy said, passing Honey the syrup for her waffles. "We're getting married so we can live together and help one another."

"You're moving in with us?" Travis's smile shone as brightly as a Christmas-tree light.

"No, you two are moving in with me, probably on New Year's Eve if everything goes according to plan. So when you come home from visiting your grandmother in Boston, you'll have a new room, right next to Sarajane's. She'll be back in France by then, but come next summer, you two can really get to know one another."

Travis took another bite of waffle and slowly chewed it, clearly lost in speculation. "Does she play with dolls and stuff?"

"Actually, she's more into softball," Andy said with a laugh. "So you two should get along just fine. Now then, any more questions?"

Travis considered, but shook his head.

"Then finish eating. I'm anxious to get our Christmas trees up and decorated." Nicole and Ethan had invited them to find trees on their wooded acreage. They'd planned the outing for this morning.

"Are we both going to have trees?" Travis asked.

"This year we'll both have trees since we're not actually getting married until the day after Christmas," Honey answered. "But next year—"

"And every year after—" interjected Andy.

"We share?" Travis looked from one to the other of the adults.

"We share," they confirmed in unison, a reply that earned them another one of Travis's brilliant smiles.

Selecting the perfect trees proved to be much easier to do than announcing the upcoming nuptials to Nicole and Ethan. Seated in the den of their home, built on the property Albert Winter had willed to Nicole, Andy intercepted more than one signal from Honey to go ahead and share their news. Finally she gave up on him and took matters into her own hands... or rather her spoon, which she tapped lightly on her mug of hot chocolate to get everyone's attention.

"Andy has an announcement to make," she told everyone and gave her dumbstruck fiancé a smile.

"Oh, um, yeah, I do," he stammered, cheeks heating. He cleared his throat, marveling that such good news should be so difficult to make...especially to friends. "We... that is, Honey and I... are getting married."

Stunned silence followed his proclamation. Then Nicole squealed, leaped from her chair and caught Honey in a hug. "I knew it! I knew it!" she exclaimed, releasing Honey and whirling to grab Andy. "Didn't I tell you, Ethan? Didn't I?"

"You did," her husband replied, patiently waiting for Nicole to step away from Andy so he could shake his hand. That formality finally accomplished, he grinned at his wife. "When was it... a week... two weeks ago?"

Honey's eyes rounded with visible astonishment. "You guessed two weeks ago that Andy and I would be getting married?" she asked Nicole.

Nicole smiled and nodded. "I *knew* two weeks ago. Why, you both glow with love every time you're together. Oh, Honey, I'm so happy for the two of you." She hugged Honey again, hard, an embrace that Honey returned, but with less enthusiasm, Andy thought. He could guess why. Honey undoubtedly felt as deceitful as he did.

"When's the wedding?" Ethan asked.

"December 26," Honey told him, extricating herself from Nicole, who then joined her husband on the couch. Behind them, logs crackled and glowed in the fireplace. "A small ceremony. Just close friends and family."

"Where?" Nicole asked, her voice muffled a bit by the mug of steaming cocoa she sipped.

"My living room," Andy answered, then added, "If I get that darned fireplace finished in time, that is."

"Why don't you have it here, instead?" Nicole suggested, belatedly glancing at Ethan as though for concurrence. "We have that formal living room we never use, and it's already decorated for Christmas...."

"Oh, I couldn't ask you to do that," Honey protested.

"You didn't ask me," Nicole said. "I volunteered. This way you two lovebirds can concentrate on what really counts—each other."

Lovebirds? Andy squirmed at the misnomer and took note of Honey's flushed cheeks. She would not meet his gaze, a sure sign Nicole's misconceptions bothered her as much as they bothered him. "Can we discuss it and get back to you?"

"Of course." Nicole gave him a smile, then turned her attention to the youngsters, sprawled on the floor. "Who wants to toast marshmallows over the fire?"

"I do! I do!" they chorused, scrambling up to follow Nicole to the kitchen. Chuckling, Ethan followed them out the door.

Alone with Honey for the moment, Andy walked over to her chair and dropped to one knee in front of her. "You okay?"

"No," she answered, massaging her temples as though she was nursing a headache. "I feel so...so dirty. Like I've just lied to my best friend."

"That's because you *have* just lied to your best friend," Andy answered. "And so have I. But we could hardly tell them the truth."

"No. They're so much in love with each other that they'd never understand." Her troubled gaze locked with his. "We *are* doing the right thing, aren't we?"

"For us, we are," Andy said. He closed the inches between them and dropped a kiss on her lips. "Love's highly overrated as a prerequisite to marriage. We both know that."

Honey nodded solemnly. "Yes."

"I need you in my life."

"I need you in mine."

"Then we're doing the right thing, honey." She smiled at him for a moment, a smile she obviously forced, then Andy kissed her again. "Now what about the wedding? Want to have it here?"

"Nicole's living room is huge," Honey said.

"Yeah," Andy agreed with a laugh, standing. "And it doesn't have a half-finished fireplace in it."

"No..." Honey's smile came more naturally this time. Andy could tell.

"So what do you say?"

"I...just don't know. I mean...Nicole thinks we're in love. It just doesn't seem right to get married in her house under such false pretenses."

Andy sighed. "I need you. I care about you. I respect you. I desire you. I want to be Daddy to your child. Isn't that enough?"

To his horror, Honey's eyes filled with tears, one of which spilled over and trailed down her cheek. "It's more than enough, Andy. More, even, than I ever hoped for, and I want you to know that I need, care about, respect and desire you, too. I can hardly wait to be Mommy to Sarajane. I always hoped I'd have a daughter someday."

"So we'll have the wedding here?"

"Yes."

"Good." Bending down, he kissed away that stray tear. "We have nothing to be ashamed of, Honey."

"I know that."

"So stop worrying."

"I will. I promise."

As though on cue, Nicole and crew burst back into the den, two bags of marshmallows and several straightened coat hangers in hand. She herded the children to the fireplace, where she and Ethan supervised, preparing the sweet treats for toasting.

"Nicole?"

Nicole glanced at Honey over the children's heads. "Hmm?"

"Andy and I have been talking and, well, we'd like to take you up on your very gracious offer."

"You'll have the wedding here?"

Honey nodded. "If you haven't had second thoughts, that is."

"Are you kidding? What better place to get married than a house built on love."

Andy tensed at Nicole's wording and shifted his gaze to Honey, fully expecting to find his fiancée disconcerted or even upset again. But Honey just winked at him, an action that laid to rest the doubts he secretly harbored but hadn't shared with her.

Their marriage *was* going to work—not because it was based on love, but because it wasn't.

That afternoon found Travis, Andy and Honey up to their knees in ornaments, lights and tinsel. They set up her tree first—a pine so tall it had to be trimmed so that Travis could, with Andy's assistance, place the star on top. Decorating it took over an hour to accomplish, after which time the three of them drove to a picturesque café, where they indulged in a tasty blue-plate special.

As she ate, Honey listened to the banter of her two favorite men and, not for the first time, thanked her lucky stars she'd found Andy. With love or without, their marriage would be a good one. And secure in that knowledge, she buried once and for all any unspoken doubts that still threatened her happiness.

For that reason, she especially enjoyed putting up and decorating Andy's Christmas tree after lunch. This being the second tree trimming of the day, the trio had the task down to a science. Andy strung the lights; Honey hung the fragile glass ornaments; Travis wound the garland and, this time, set an angel on top.

Just as Andy reached to plug in the lights, the phone rang. Both Honey and Travis groaned at the delay, so it was a chuckling Andy who answered it.

"Hello? Yes. This is Andy Fulbright." Honey, busy rearranging ornaments so there wouldn't be any bare spots, paid little attention to her fiancé until she heard him blurt, "Jaclyn...what's up?" She turned, then, and saw Andy frowning into the phone. "What do you mean

Sarajane won't be coming in on the twenty-second? You promised me. You can't back out now...."

Oh, no, Honey silently groaned as Andy continued to rave at his ex. He'd been so looking forward to seeing his daughter. What was Jaclyn trying to do to him?

"And besides that, I already have her plane ticket to Alabama. You know how hard they are to get this time of year. I—what's that?" He winced. "All right... all right. You can talk now." Andy positively scowled into the phone, an expression that, to Honey's astonishment, soon softened and then actually blossomed into a smile right before her eyes. "I'll meet her in New York, then... same as always?"

Another long silence, during which Andy grinned, nodded and held out an arm to Honey. She abandoned the tree and went to him at once, slipping her arms around his waist, offering support if he needed it, though from all appearances he didn't.

"All right. I'll be there... and thanks, Jaclyn. This is great... a wonderful surprise." A moment later, Andy dropped the receiver into the cradle and wrapped his other arm around Honey, whom he hugged without mercy.

"What is it?" she gasped, unable to contain her curiosity one moment longer. She felt him trembling with what appeared to be excitement. "What's happened?"

"A change of plans," Andy replied, releasing her. "Sarajane's coming on the nineteenth." He drew in a shaky breath that would have revealed the extent of his joy if his tears hadn't already. "Extra days with my daughter, a new wife and son. This is a miracle I didn't expect." He swallowed hard and shook his head, clearly self-conscious about his emotion.

"This is going to be the best Christmas ever," Honey agreed, framing his face with her hands, kissing him on the chin. She turned to Travis. "Did you hear that? Sarajane's coming earlier."

"Neat-o," Travis responded, his mouth stained red from a candy cane that should have been hung on the tree.

Honey and Andy exchanged a look, then laughed. He plugged in the tree lights, illuminating their handiwork—an awesome sight that warmed Honey's heart almost as much as Andy's jubilant smile.

The tree finally finished, the three of them retired to Andy's kitchen where Honey supervised the making of fudge and peanut brittle. Travis soon tired of the fun and became more of a pest than a help, so he was allowed to explore this house that would soon be his home. Andy, however, stayed until the last pan and spoon were washed, talking nonstop about his daughter the whole time.

It was Sarajane this and Sarajane that, and while thrilled for him, Honey experienced an unexplainable twinge of something akin to fear. Even more baffling was her feeling of being left out. Why, they weren't even married yet. How could she feel left out?

Was it because he so obviously adored his daughter? Undoubtedly, Honey decided, amazed by her roller-coaster emotions. Surely she didn't want to be the object of such devotion herself. Surely that wasn't why she felt so neglected . . . so, yes, *jealous*.

Shame on you, Honey Truman, Honey silently scolded. That dressing down didn't help, though, and by nightfall her Christmas spirit had drooped decidedly. If jealousy had, indeed, compromised her good cheer, then she had problems . . . big problems. To be jealous of another female—even this pint-size female—a woman had to love the man they had in common. Did this mean that she, Honorine Truman, loved Andy?

Heaven forbid, Honey thought, but it was with difficulty that she put the notion out of her head and survived the rest of that long day.

Alone in his bed that night—but not for many more—Andy whispered a prayer of thanks that he'd found Honey and Travis, that Sarajane would have extra days in the States, and that he'd actually managed to exchange his December 22 flight to New York for an earlier one. So what if it was a red-eye on the eighteenth? And so what if he hadn't been able to swap their December 23 tickets to Alabama? He had no problems with the idea of bumming around New York With Sarajane for a few days other than wishing the two of them could spend the time with Honey and Travis, preparing for the wedding.

But the ceremony really was going to be a simple one, and Honey had assured him that she and Nicole could easily handle the few details it entailed. Besides, he'd be back in Alabama three whole days before the wedding, so could help with last-minute preparations. And it wasn't as though he wouldn't be taking care of a few wedding details of his own—details such as buying Sarajane a bridesmaid's dress and Honey a ring.

A ring... With a start, Andy realized he had no idea what kind of ring Honey wanted. For that reason, he asked her the next time he saw her on Monday morning.

"Just get a plain gold band," Honey replied. Arms loaded with books, she walked from her office to the room next door, where Andy's shelves now lined the walls and crisscrossed the floor. "That would be—

oomph!—the easiest thing to do." Relieved of the books, which now lay piled on a table, she dusted off her hands and turned her full attention to him.

Andy stole a moment to appreciate her rainbow colored sweater before responding. "You don't like diamonds?"

"I love diamonds. I hate decisions," she replied, slipping past to return to her office.

Andy followed. "Does that mean you wouldn't mind if *I* made the decision."

"I'd be eternally grateful," Honey said from behind her desk. "Now I hate to run you off, but—"

"You have work to do?"

She grinned. "Exactly. And so do you if we're going to manage time off for a honeymoon."

"I do plan on one of those," Andy said, moving from the door to the desk. He planted his hands on it and towered over where she sat looking as demure as the old-maid librarian he'd once imagined. How long ago that seemed now...an eternity almost. Andy found it hard to believe there was a time when Honey hadn't brightened his life. He could barely recall those lonely days, thanks to this woman, and on that thought gave her a kiss of heartfelt gratitude.

"I lo—" Just in time, Andy caught the words of love that seemed to hover on the tip of his tongue these days, just waiting to slip out. Not for the first time, he marveled at how readily those three little words sprang to mind when he kissed Honey. And not for the first time, he told himself they resulted from instinct or maybe old habits. Most often, kisses did mean love.

Unfortunately, they didn't now.

Unfortunately?

"What did you say?" Honey murmured, her words muffled by his mouth, still touching hers.

"I, um, like your sweater."

Honey pulled back and glanced down at the garment. "Isn't it great? I got it on sale a few months ago and just now got around to wearing it."

"That's nice," Andy said absently, his mind not on the sweater, but on the state of his emotions. *Unfortunately?* Did he really think it unfortunate that Honey and he weren't in love? "I'm going now."

"See ya." She dismissed him with a wave and a smile.

Turning on his heel, Andy sped down the hall and out the back door to his "shop," where he sucked in the crisp winter air and tried, for the umpteenth time, to assess his feelings for Honey.

Did he . . . or did he *not* . . . love Honey? he asked himself. Andy first considered his physical state when he was around her—ready and willing. But who needed love to feel passion? Not Andy Fulbright or many other men.

Andy next considered his emotional state when he was with Honey—protective of her, sensitive to her. In short, he cared, a feeling he'd already admitted to Honey, a feeling that was a far cry from love.

Well . . . maybe not *that* far, but far enough that he could marry without fear of being hurt again. And that's what mattered, of course. That's what was most important. Not getting hurt . . . not hurting anyone else.

Tuesday, Wednesday and Thursday flew by, a whirlwind of activities that ranged from a Christmas parade downtown to a surprise bridal shower, hosted by Nicole and Ethan, that lasted right up until he left Winterhaven for the Birmingham airport, around eight o'clock Thursday night.

Andy drove alone to the airport, which bustled with holiday travelers. He loved the contagious excitement in the air. He hated the long lines at every ticket counter and security check. But a glance out one of the many windows revealed a sky studded with stars—perfect weather for flying—and that observation settled his stomach, churning in anticipation of seeing Sarajane in a matter of hours.

Upon his arrival in New York, early Friday morning, Andy went straight to the hotel in which he'd reserved the room he and his daughter would stay in until they departed for home the following Wednesday. Flopping across the bed, Andy closed his eyes and indulged himself in renewed frustration that the two of them would have to spend so many days in New York even though he knew they wouldn't be a total waste. He'd make the most of this time with his daughter after being so long apart, then be all the more eager to fly home to marry the woman he loved—

"Damn!" Andy suddenly exclaimed, then, and only then, realizing that the L word had slipped into his thoughts *again.* Unbelievable! And darned disconcerting...so disconcerting, in fact, that Andy sprang off the bed and strode to the door, fully intent on finding some breakfast, taking a walk, buying a present, or otherwise distracting himself from the insanity of falling for Honey...assuming it wasn't too late.

Assuming he didn't love her already.

Eight o'clock Saturday found Andy back in the bustling airport, anxiously awaiting Sarajane's plane and still denying he loved Honey. With hammering heart, he watched his daughter's plane land. With knotted stomach, he and several hundred other folks crowded the walkway where the passengers would arrive. The minutes ticked by, the door finally opened, strangers streamed through it and quickly dispersed into the waiting crush. All around him, Andy heard the sounds of joy and laughter. Impatiently he scanned the disembarking passengers for a glimpse of his daughter.

Had she changed very much since last he'd seen her? he wondered. Was she all grown-up. . . a little lady? But of course not, he chided himself. She was still only six and small for her age. That's why he trained his gaze just about knee-high to the rest of the travelers.

"Daddy! Daddy!"

Andy saw her the very instant she shouted his name. In a flash, he snatched her up in his arms and hugged her with all the joy of a man kept waiting far too long.

"Hello, Andy."

Andy tensed at the sound of that familiar voice, only belatedly realizing that someone—an unexpected someone—was standing nearby.

"Jaclyn. What are you doing here?" Andy's ex-wife had never accompanied her daughter before. He glanced worriedly at his daughter, who appeared to be healthy, but must be dreadfully ill for her busy mother to have come along. "What is it? What's wrong?"

"Nothing's wrong," Jaclyn quickly assured him with a toss of shimmering blond hair. "I need to talk to you, and it's not a conversation I trust to an overseas operator."

"I. . . well, uh, all right," Andy stammered, still stunned and more than a little uneasy. "My hotel is only thirty minutes away. Shall we go there?"

"No. I'm flying back in an hour. How about one of the restaurants? Or, better still, can't we just find a bench somewhere close by? I'd like to get this over with as quickly as possible."

Over with? What the hell...? "Yeah...sure." He glanced around, located a relatively empty waiting area and led the way. After setting Sarajane on one of the vinyl seats and handing her the present he'd brought along, Andy and Jaclyn stepped just out of earshot, a few feet away. "What's up, Jackie?"

"A change in plans," Jaclyn replied, her voice low. "A big change."

Andy tensed and glared at his ex-wife, instantly recalling the last time she'd prefaced a conversation with those words. "Where are you and Jean moving to now?"

"Oh, we're not moving, but we are filming on location in India come January and—"

"India!"

"Yes, and I—"

"You're taking Sarajane to India? But what about her school, her friends? And how will this affect her time with me next summer?"

Jaclyn threw her hands up in obvious exasperation, a gesture Andy knew well since they'd often disagreed. "If you'll hush for one minute, I'll tell you."

"I'm listening."

"We're going to be moving around a lot... Bombay...Madras...Bangalore. It will be hard on us. It will be impossible for Sarajane. I'm here today to ask if you'll take her full-time until we return to France—a year, maybe eighteen months in all."

Chapter Ten

"What did you say? Andy, Andy, please slow down. I can't understand a word you're saying," Honey scolded, laughing into the phone at her fiancé, who positively babbled about something and from New York's JFK airport, no less!

"Jaclyn and Jean... that's her husband... are filming on location in India. I'm going to have Sarajane *for a whole year*... maybe more!"

Instantly Honey's knees turned to jelly. In a state of shock, she sagged against her kitchen counter, strewn with the salad makings that were going to be her lunch. "That's wonderful!"

"Yeah. God, I hate this delay. I want to fly home today... now... so we can get started on this time together. It's going to be great, Honey. It's going to be perfect!"

"Yes...yes...it is," Honey agreed, even as her stomach knotted with the certainty that it *wasn't* going to be perfect at all.

Not that she wasn't ecstatic for Andy, she candidly acknowledged minutes later when he finally rang off after telling her about the weather in New York—a blizzard—and asking about the weather in Winterhaven—rain, rain, rain. She knew what this meant to him...she really did. Nonetheless she wondered what this change would mean to them—her and Andy—and their relationship, based as it was on need and not on love.

A man with a daughter wouldn't *need* a companion as much as a man without a daughter...would he? And if Andy no longer *needed* Honey or Travis to be happy, would he not now have second thoughts about marrying again? Honey's eyes brimmed at the mere idea of losing Andy—an intense emotional reaction that left her trembling and absolutely certain she finally, *finally* knew the answer to the question that had haunted her for weeks now: did she love Andy Fulbright?

Yes! Yes! Yes!

"But he doesn't love me back," Honey wailed, bursting into tears, and sinking into one of the nearby kitchen chairs. Luckily Travis wasn't home to witness her weepy wallow in self-pity.

What a mess! What a gosh-awful mess. In exactly one week she would be walking down the aisle with Andy—a man who'd never loved her and now didn't even need her. Would he still want to tie the knot? she worried. And, more importantly, if he didn't want to, would he have the guts to confess?

Or would he marry her, anyway, out of some misguided desire to save face, or maybe out of Southern male gallantry or, worst of all, out of pity? Honey sobbed noisily at the thought, chewing her nails, leaping up to pace the colorful linoleum floor. What to do...what to do...

Many minutes ticked by on her wall clock before she finally reached any sort of conclusion. Short of breaking off the engagement herself—and there was no way she could bring herself to do that!—Honey had no option but to keep her eyes and ears open for any change in Andy's behavior toward her and Travis once he returned to Alabama.

She would listen, not only to the words he said, but to the tone in which he said them. Truth or lie? she'd ask herself every time he spoke. She would watch and analyze his every move; she'd read his body language. Did he really want to hold her, kiss her? Or did he hold a part of himself back?

It wouldn't be easy, this second-guessing, but Honey intended to do it...right up to the hour of the wedding. She had no choice if she wanted to save Andy—and herself—from what they both needed least: another disastrous marriage.

"I like that one there," Sarajane told her father Monday afternoon after a full day's worth of seeking just the right wedding ring for Honey. They stood outside Tiffany's, staring through a spotless plate-glass window at a sparkling display of jewelry.

"Which?" Andy asked, a bit overwhelmed by the sight of all that black velvet and ice. He'd examined at least a zillion rings the past couple of days. They'd begun to look the same to him, so much so that the plain gold band suggested by Honey seemed a refreshing alternative, if the easy way out of this dilemma.

"That one there," Sarajane, still bubbling with energy, repeated. She touched her gloved forefinger to the glass as though that might help.

It didn't, so Andy took a wild guess. "The marquise?"

"No," replied his daughter, who by now knew the lingo as well as he. "The heart one."

Andy spied it at once—an exquisite solitaire. He frowned uncertainly at his offspring, her face almost obscured by fuzzy blue earmuffs. "You think I should buy a heart-shaped diamond?"

"Of course," she replied, taking his hand and tugging him against the bitter winter wind to the front entrance. "Hearts mean love, and you love Honey a whole, whole bunch."

"Yes, but—" Abruptly, Andy stopped short, a move that yanked his eager daughter, in the bright red car coat, right off her feet and back into his arms. Absently he righted her. Yes? He'd actually said *yes* in answer to this innocent question from a child—to whom he'd never, ever lie?

"Whasamatter, Daddy? Don't you want to go inside and buy this bee-you-teeful ring?" She stomped her fur-lined boots against the pavement, no doubt to keep her toes from freezing.

"Sure, sure," Andy murmured, shaking his head in bemusement that it had taken him so very long to face up to a truth that friends and relatives had known all along. "I want to buy the ring." But would Honey want to wear a heart-shaped diamond that symbolized, of all things, love?

"Then what's wrong?"

More than you'll ever know, Andy silently answered, already plotting ways to make Honey love him back. It wouldn't be easy, dead set against that emotion as she was. But he'd try...oh, how he'd try... beginning with their I do's on the twenty-sixth. Until then, he'd play it cool of necessity so as not to scare her off.

Honey heard the telephone ringing when she parked in her driveway around five o'clock on December 22. Certain that it was Andy, finally home from New York, she bypassed the muddy path to her front porch, instead entering through the seldom-used back entrance. Maneuvering her way through the still-unpacked boxes lining the laundry room, she burst into the kitchen, Travis on her heels, and snatched up the receiver of the wall phone.

"Hello?" Pant. Pant.

"Honey, it's Andy."

Honey nodded happy confirmation to Travis, who now hovered at her elbow. He immediately grinned from ear to ear and stomped his feet in joy. "Well, it's about time you got home, stranger! How was New York?"

"New York's too cold, too crowded and not where I want to be tonight, but I'm still here, anyway."

"Still... You mean you're not in Winterhaven?"

"No." Honey heard the weariness and frustration in Andy's voice. "We're iced in. Until tomorrow, at least."

"Oh, babe, I'm so sorry."

"Not half as sorry as me. I know you're up to your neck in wedding plans, and I feel terrible that I'm not there to help."

Is that the only reason you wish you were home? Honey instantly wondered. Don't you miss us at all? "It's okay. I understand." And I'm so grateful a wedding is still on your agenda whether you miss us or not.

"It's not okay. It's—" He broke off abruptly, and Honey heard him talking to someone, probably his daughter, in muffled tones. "Are you there, Honey? Sarajane says she wants to talk to you."

"I'm here."

"Miss Honey?" It was Sarajane, sounding six-year-old sweet.

"Hi, Sarajane. How are you?"

"Fine. I'm glad you're gonna marry my daddy."

"So am I," Honey replied from the heart. "Are you going to be in our wedding?"

Sarajane sighed with a definite lack of enthusiasm. "Only if I don't have to wear a stupid ol' dress that makes me trip."

Honey heard Andy's groan off in the background and had to laugh, now feeling better than she had in a while. "How about a short dress? Would you wear one of those?"

"Will I have to stick flowers in my hair?" Clearly Sarajane was remembering her mother's last nuptials, which, according to Andy, had been much too elegant for his tastes.

"No flowers," Honey solemnly informed her. "We're keeping things simple."

"Then I guess a short dress will be okay."

"Good. Now may I speak to your daddy again for a minute?"

"Uh-huh." Again Honey heard the muffled tones of a conversation, the "short dress" part of which came through loud and clear.

"Thanks," Andy said. "I'll use this weather delay to good advantage and find her a short dress—" he chuckled "—tonight."

"I thought you'd have taken care of that little detail days ago," Honey teasingly scolded. "What have you been doing with your time?"

"Shopping for something equally important," came Andy's cryptic reply, and no matter how Honey prodded, he wouldn't say anything else.

Honey heard not another word from him, but didn't worry...until her phone rang midafternoon on Wednesday, December 23.

"At last!" she exclaimed, pretending to race her son to the phone. Since her Christmas holiday had officially begun that morning, the two of them had spent the day baking, shopping and otherwise whiling away the hours until Andy got back to town.

"It's him! It's him!" Travis exclaimed, thrusting the receiver into Honey's waiting hands. His joy, while a wondrous thing to witness, worried her more than she cared to admit. What if Andy had changed toward the child after all these days with his own offspring? Such a reaction would be understandable... natural even.

"You're home," she breathed into the receiver.

"We're not," Andy snapped back, the next second apologizing. "Sorry about that, but if you've watched the weather at all this week, you must know we're in the middle of the worst winter storm in years."

Honey's spirits plunged to her shoelaces. "I'm so sorry, Andy. I know you're sick of the city by now."

"And then some," Andy admitted with a lusty sigh. "I've hung around the airport so long, I'm on a first-name basis with the pilots. One of them told me we'd be lucky to get out of here before Christmas. I just hope we don't have to postpone the wedding."

Postpone the wedding? Honey's blood ran cold as all her recent insecurities and fears returned in a sudden rush. Was that the reason for all this delay? she wondered, the next moment blushing with shame for her irrational suspicions. Disconcerted, she tried to change the subject.

"I think I'd better tell you that Sarajane's grandparents called today and invited me to stop by their house on Christmas Eve. Seems they're having a bunch of relatives over to see you both as a surprise. I told her I'd try to come, but I must admit I have no intentions of going unless you're with me."

"I'll try to make it," Andy softly promised, words that should have consoled, but instead made Honey shiver anew in apprehension.

Christmas Eve dawned rainy, cold and as gloomy as Honey's spirits. Not a moment passed that day without a thought about Andy. Would he make it home in time for the grandparents' surprise party, for Christmas, *for their wedding?*

Of necessity, she and Travis had spent many hours away from home taking care of last-minute shopping for the wedding and his impending trip to Boston. Honey tried not to think about that trip, which would take place whether or not she married. She knew that if Andy backed out and Travis left town at the same time, she would find herself, chin-deep and still sinking, in a blue Christmas funk the likes of which no songwriter had ever imagined, much less immortalized. It didn't help that Travis asked every five minutes when Andy would be home.

By five-thirty that evening, after a long day without any word from Andy, Honey hit rock bottom. By now convinced that Andy wasn't going to make it home, *period,* she dressed her son and herself in warm clothing, then drove to the town square to join the community carolers.

Famous throughout the town for spreading holiday cheer, the group visited the nursing home and numerous homebound citizens every year. Honey knew there was no better way to put her problems in perspective than to be around folks with worse ones.

For that reason, she wasn't home when Andy tried to call her from his ex-in-laws' house around six-forty-five that evening. He had no idea where she'd gone, of course, an irritation that only compounded his current frustration. Finally back in Winterhaven after much too long away, he had better things to do than listen to Uncle Whatsit and Aunt Whoever tell Sarajane how much she'd grown.

But he did what he had to do, leaving messages on Honey's machine every half hour until eight o'clock, when she answered the phone at last. "It's about time you got home!" he exclaimed, vastly relieved and not a little thrilled to hear her voice.

"I could say the same to you," Honey replied, "assuming you *are* home."

"I am . . . thank God." She sounded so wonderful, he had to blink back tears. *Steady, Andy. She doesn't know what's going on.* "Are you coming to the party?"

"Sounds like you're having fun, but I think that if Travis and I go anywhere else tonight, it'll be to Christmas Eve services."

"May Sarajane and I join you? We'll surely be finished up here in another hour or so. Or will that be too late?"

"Service begins at ten o'clock. Come to the back door of the house."

"Oh, we'll be there long before that," Andy promised, so distracted he didn't register her comment about the back door enough to even wonder about it. "By nine at the latest."

But it was actually after that before he finally managed to steal his daughter from her loving grandparents and then only because he blurted an invitation for them to come to his house early the next morning to watch Sarajane open her presents. Andy and his exhausted daughter had managed to make it halfway to his truck when a fresh carload of relatives from out of state pulled into the driveway and dragged him and his precious bundle back into the house.

Andy called Honey the first chance he got, noting that she sounded a bit cool this time. But who could blame her? He was at his wit's end, dying to hold her, kiss her.

"I'll be there before ten," he therefore promised. "Not a minute later."

At ten-fifteen, Andy wheeled his truck into Honey's driveway. He found her house dark, her car missing—sure indications she'd given up on him and gone on to church alone. Andy toyed with the idea of joining her there, late or not, but quickly abandoned that notion when Sarajane began to whine that she was tired and wanted to go home *now*.

So much for seeing Honey tonight, he thought, immediately telling himself it was just as well. In his present state of pent-up desire, he might do something really stupid such as blurt out his love.

In the end, Andy settled on writing a note, asking her to call him the moment she got home, no matter how late it was. Never once remembering her advice about the back door, he stuck the note on the front door, where he knew she'd be sure to see it.

* * *

Still humming "O Holy Night," her favorite Christmas carol, Honey pulled into her driveway just after midnight. Bypassing the muddy front yard, just as she'd done all week, she walked around back with her sleeping son—who was quite a bundle these days!—in her arms. On that door she found, apparently undisturbed, the note she'd written to Andy when he hadn't shown up by ten o'clock. Refusing to let his actions, or lack of them, upset her again, Honey tucked in her son, took a quick shower and then crawled into her own bed.

But sleep eluded her. It seemed her worst fears were reality. Now that Andy had Sarajane back, he didn't need a divorced librarian and her son to keep him busy. And to think she'd once thought herself so clever to marry out of need instead of for love....

What a mistake. Love was truly the tie that made a forever possible between a woman and a man. Without that bond, that permanence, any marriage was a bad gamble at best.

The sound of the doorbell woke Andy from a too-sound sleep Christmas morning. Inordinately startled and more than a little disoriented when he leaped up, he forgot where he was—the couch in the living room—and so stumbled smack into the wall that would've been a door if he'd slept in his bed.

Now wide-awake and groaning, he hurried to open the front door and found Sarajane's grandparents standing on his porch. Their wide eyes told him what a mess he must look, and after trying to explain how he'd fallen asleep waiting for a telephone call, Andy made a beeline to his bedroom, where he showered, shaved and dressed in record time.

That accomplished, he listened for Sarajane—and heard not a peep from her—then snatched the telephone and punched out Honey's number. "Why didn't you call me last night?" he demanded the moment she answered the phone.

"What are you talking about?" Honey replied, her tone almost cool.

"I left you a note, asking you to call the minute you got home from church."

"You came by last night?" Cool had turned cold—very cold.

"Of course I did," he said, somewhat defensively. "Just after ten. You weren't there."

"Of course I wasn't," she retorted, mimicking his tone exactly. "You were late."

"I got hung up with Sarajane's kin. You know how demanding big families can be."

"Actually, I don't."

Honey sounded angry now...really angry...and was certainly justified in feeling that way if she hadn't had much dealing with Southern kith and kin. "I'm sorry, okay?" Andy blurted out. "I'm sorry, and I'm dying to see you."

"So come over now. We won't open another present until you get here, and I'll even cook breakfast for you and Sarajane."

Well, hell! "Honey, I'm sorry but Jaclyn's mom and dad are here right this minute, so we can't come now. We will, though. Just as soon as they leave."

A long silence followed. "I guess we'll see you when we see you then, huh?"

"I swear it won't be long," Andy told her and was rewarded for his promise by a click that told him she'd heard that story one time too many the past few hours.

"He's here! He's really, truly here!" Travis yelled just over an hour later.

Honey tried to muster a smile in response to her son's excitement, but failed miserably. How could she be happy in the face of such an uncertain future?

Andy and Sarajane burst into the living room a short time later, bringing with them a swirl of chilly air. He looked so wonderful, Honey wished they could go back in time to a couple of weeks ago when she felt free to hold and kiss him. Today, she felt none of that freedom, and actually stiffened when he reached for her.

He sensed the change. She could tell, and so was not surprised when he shepherded her to the kitchen right after introductions. "What's wrong?" he demanded at once, backing her against the wall, holding her there with his hands planted to the wall on either side of her head. "Are you still angry about last night?"

"I'm not angry," she answered truthfully. Sad, regretful, miserable... these were far better adjectives.

"Then kiss me."

Honey did—a brief, brushing caress that was all she dared allow herself. More might give away her love for him, and that was a humiliation she could not bear.

"What's wrong?" he repeated when she pulled back again.

"Nothing," Honey lied. How could she admit to her jealousy, her insecurity, her disappointment that there would be no wedding? These were emotions that would reveal her feelings for him even more clearly than any confession. As for just plain telling him the truth...well, that was out of the question.

Andy stood in silence for a moment, his gaze nailing her to the wall. "Does this have anything to do with Sarajane?" he finally demanded.

"What do you mean?"

"I mean, are you upset because my daughter will be here with us all the time? It's a lot of responsibility. Maybe more than you planned on—"

Honey's jaw dropped. "How can you say such a thing?" she snapped, ducking under his arms to put distance between them. Only belatedly did she realize the full implication of the accusation. "You mean...you still want to marry me?"

This time it was Andy's jaw that dropped. "What the hell are you talking about? Of course I want to marry you. Why would you think I wouldn't?"

Honey, overwhelmed with relief and the love she dared not confess, sat down hard on the nearest chair. "Because now that Sarajane's here, you don't need Travis or me anymore." She swiped angrily at a telltale tear. "I'll really understand if you don't want to go through with this wedding thing, you know. I mean...I won't make you marry me."

"Make me? Damn, Honey. I was only out of town a week. How on earth did things get so screwed up between us?"

"I don't know," she replied with a sniff and a helpless shrug that brought him to his knees—literally—right in front of her.

"Sarajane! Travis!" he suddenly yelled. "Get in here."

They did, panting from the race.

"Are you...gonna...give it to her now?" Sarajane demanded breathlessly, her eyes glowing with what could only be excitement.

"Give her what?" Travis asked. He looked as confused as Honey felt.

"This," Andy replied, pulling what looked to be a ring box out of the pocket of his sheepskin jacket. With a heart-melting smile, he handed it to her.

And with trembling hands, Honey raised the lid to find a heart-shaped diamond solitaire.

"Oh, my..." she breathed. She took it from the box and held it out so the children could see how it glittered. Instantly, the diamond prism caught the light and spangled the ceiling.

"Sarajane picked it out," Andy said, slipping the ring onto her finger.

"I chose a heart," his daughter solemnly explained, "'cause hearts mean love, and my daddy loves you *so much.*"

Loves me so much? Fat chance, Honey thought, nonetheless helpless to keep from glancing at Andy as though he might actually confirm Sarajane's words.

"I—I know this wasn't part of our deal..." he stammered to her astonishment, instead of winking or otherwise acknowledging their old conspiracy.

Honey caught her breath. "What...?"

Andy nodded slowly. "It's true. I love you."

"Oh, my God." She closed her eyes, fighting the tears of joy that threatened to flow.

"Now don't even think of backing out on this wedding. I know my loving you is unexpected, but it doesn't have to be fatal. It's me taking the risk, after all. Nothing's changed as far as you're concerned...."

"That's what you think," Honey softly interjected, words that took a moment to register with her flustered fiancé.

When they did, his eyes rounded in absolute shock. "What are you saying to me?"

"I'm saying I love you, too."

"Holy—" At once, Honey found herself on her feet and crushed to Andy. Heart-to-heart they stood for long moments, oblivious to the whispered plotting of their mischievous offspring. "When did you know?" Andy asked, his voice low and for her ears only.

"I've suspected it for weeks. I've only known for sure a couple of days. What about you?"

"Same problem. Suspected it forever. Figured it out while I was in New York." He chuckled, a warm, throaty sound that sent shivers of desire skittering down Honey's arms. "Can you believe we've been so dense?"

"No," she answered with a soft laugh.

He sighed and held her tighter. "Do you think our marriage would've worked...if we really hadn't fallen in love, I mean?"

"I don't know," Honey admitted. "I thought so at the time, but now that I love you...now that I know how special things can be, I can't imagine how we ever believed it could."

Childish giggling gradually brought them back to reality—giggling and Sarajane's urgent, "Look up, Daddy...look up."

Andy, still lost in love, barely heard and so didn't obey.

"Dad-dy! Can't you hear me? *Look up!*"

With a start, Andy did, and found mistletoe dangling over their heads thanks to Travis, precariously balanced on one of the kitchen chairs just behind his blushing mom.

"Now give her a kiss," Sarajane sternly instructed her slow-witted parent. "A great big Christmas kiss she'll never, ever forget."

With a grin, Andy eagerly obeyed.

A dad didn't always have to be told twice.

* * * * *